Praise for the EMILY WINDSNAP novels

'An absolutely enchanting debut – a salty splash of something fresh'
Amanda Craig

'. . . enchanting fantasy from a striking new voice'
Publishing News

'The wonders of this world are described in detail, from the colours of the mermaid tails to the glowing magic of the oral reef'
School Library Journal

'. . . a superb pre-teen read . . . girls will love this . . . since it's not just full of adventure and fantastical whimsy, but also has moving undertones of family and friendship throughtout'
Waterstones Books Quarterly

'Light-hearted and exciting . . . rich, descriptive passages, unusual in a story for this age group, conjure a vast watery world . . . inhabited by shadowy creatures'
Books for Keeps

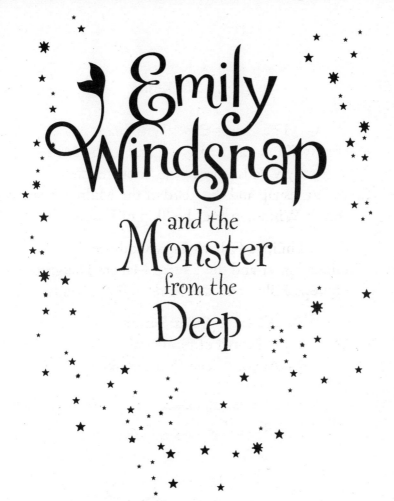

Emily Windsnap and the Monster from the Deep

LIZ KESSLER

Decorations by Sarah Gibb

Orion
Children's Books

First published in Great Britain in 2004
by Orion Children's Books
Paperback edition first published in 2005 by Dolphin Paperbacks
This edition published in 2012 by Orion Children's Books
Reissued in 2015 by Orion Children's Books
an imprint of Hachette Children's Group
a division of Hodder and Stoughton Limited

Carmelite House
50 Victoria Embankment
London EC4V ODZ
An Hachette UK Company

1 3 5 7 9 10 8 6 4 2

A catalogue record for this book is available from the British Library.

ISBN: 978 1 4440 1510 2

Typeset by Input Data Services Ltd, Bridgwater, Somerset

Printed in Great Britain by Clays Ltd, St Ives plc

www.orionchildrensbooks.com

*For Hannah, Barney, Katie
. . . and Mum*

Once again, I can't claim to have done this all on my own. Lots of people have been involved in the process. I would especially like to thank:

Jeanette, Andrew, Alex and Amber, for two incredible weeks in Bermuda;

Ben and Sam, for the day out on the pirate ship (even if it didn't go anywhere);

Fiz, for sharing so many special moments, and crying at most of them;

Kirsty, for being so proud and excited, and so good at sharing champagne;

Fiona and the fab team at Orion Children's Books, for being so behind Emily;

Sarah, for all the beautiful artwork;

My family and lots of other friends for all sorts of help along the way.

With extra special thanks to:

Kath, for 100% spot-on editorial feedback and for sharing the agony of second-book syndrome;

Lee, for again being a complete inspiration and a central part of helping this book to take shape;

Catherine, for doing all the right things for Emily and for me, and doing them with patience, friendship, care and skill;

And Judith, for being such a thorough and brilliant editor that all my writer-friends are jealous.

Below the thunders of the upper deep;
Far far beneath in the abysmal sea,
His ancient, dreamless, uninvaded sleep
The Kraken sleepeth ...

From 'The Kraken'
by Alfred, Lord Tennyson

Chapter One

*C*lose your eyes.
Think of the most beautiful place you can imagine.

Are you seeing golden beaches? Gorgeous clear blue sea? Perfect sky? Keep your eyes closed.

Now multiply it by about a hundred and you're halfway to picturing what my new home was like. The softest, whitest sand, palm trees that reached lazily out from the beaches, tall rocky arches cusping the bays, sea that sparkled like crystals in the sunlight. All thanks to Neptune.

He'd sent me here with my mum and dad to start a

new life. Somewhere we could live together. Somewhere my secret would be safe.

One of Neptune's guards, Archieval, accompanied us here. He's a merman. He swam beside our little sailing boat all the way, swishing his long black hair behind him and occasionally ducking under, flicking his tail in the air, silver and sharp, like a dagger.

We edged slowly into a horseshoe-shaped bay filled with shiny turquoise water. Soft foamy waves gently stroked the white sand. A few boats were dotted about in the bay, half sunken, silently sloping. Some were modern yachts, others great wooden craft that looked like ancient pirate ships.

A tall rocky arch marked the end of the bay. Through it, the sand and sea continued round a corner. I caught my breath as I stood and stared.

'Shake a tail, someone,' Archieval called up. 'I could use some help here.'

I leaned across to help him pull the boat up alongside a wooden jetty as Dad swam round to the back and tied the ropes to a buoy. Mum was still inside with Millie. That's her friend from Brightport. She used to read fortunes on the pier. She did a tarot reading for Archieval before we left and he liked it so much he invited her to come with us.

She said she'd have to let the cards decide, so she set

the pack out in a star shape and sat looking at it in silence for about ten minutes, nodding slowly.

'Well, it's obvious what I have to do. You'll never catch me ignoring a call from the ten of cups,' she said enigmatically before throwing her black cape over her shoulder and going home to pack her things. She says everything enigmatically, Millie does. I've learned to just nod and look as though I know what she's on about.

Archieval swam round to the side of the boat. 'This is it then,' he said. 'North Bay, Allpoints Island.'

'Why's it called Allpoints Island?' I asked.

'It's right in the centre of the Triangle.' He stretched out an arm as he spun slowly round in a circle. 'Where the three points meet.'

The Bermuda Triangle. I shivered. He'd told us about it on the way here, about the boats and planes that had mysteriously disappeared inside it. An ocean liner had been found totally intact but utterly deserted. Twenty tables were set out for dinner. Another ship was found with skeletons on the decks, its sails ripped to shreds all around them. Others had vanished without trace, often after frantic mayday calls from pilots and fishermen who were never seen again.

I didn't know whether to believe the stories at first, but something had happened out at sea. We'd been sailing along normally, the swell rising and falling, the boat gently making its way though the peaks and troughs. Then it changed. The water went all glassy. The engine cut out, everything died. Even my watch stopped working. It felt as if the sea had frozen, almost as if time itself had frozen.

Then Archieval yanked his long hair into a ponytail with some string and disappeared under the water. A few minutes later, we got moving again, gliding silently across the glassy sea.

'That was it,' he called up. 'Bermuda Triangle. That's what'll protect you from the outside world now. No one knows how to get through it except for a few chosen merfolk.' He threw a rope onto the deck. 'Well, a few chosen merfolk and . . . no, I'd better not tell you about that.'

'What? Tell me.'

Dad turned up then. 'I hope you're not filling my daughter's head with any more of your lurid tales, Archie,' he warned him. 'She has enough nightmares as it is.'

Archie lowered his voice. 'Just be careful,' he said. 'That glassy plane marks out the Triangle, but it's only like that on the surface. It's a raging torrent below: a huge well leading down to the deepest depths of the ocean. And you don't want to go disappearing down a hole like that.'

I rubbed at the goosepimples crawling up my arms.

We'd sailed on calmly after that, slipping through water that grew clearer and lighter every moment, melting from deep navy to a soft baby blue.

Gradually, the island came into view. It was quite

small, perhaps only a few miles across: a tall cliff at one end, a couple of lower peaks at the other and a low, flat stretch in between. As we drew closer, I could see the coastline was made up of long white bays fringed with tall palm trees and clusters of rocks and arches. It looked like a postcard. I'd always thought those pictures must be made up, somehow, and that when you got there, you'd just find a clump of high-rise apartments next to a building site.

But it was real. And it was my new home.

'Where's your dad?' Mum joined me on the deck, straightening her skirt and bending down to check her reflection in a metal railing.

I pointed ahead. 'Helping Archie.'

Mum looked slowly round the bay. 'I think I've died and gone to heaven,' she murmured as she grabbed the railing. 'Someone's going to have to pinch me.'

'I'll do it!' Dad's head poked out of the water, a glint in his eyes as he wiped floppy wet hair off his forehead. Mum smiled back at him.

A second later, the side doors crashed open and Millie clambered out. 'Tell you something,' she said, rubbing her large stomach. 'That Slippery Elm mixture works wonders on the seasickness.' She covered her mouth as she hiccupped. 'Especially washed down with a spot of brandy. Now, where are we?'

She squinted into the sunlight. 'That's it!' she said, pointing across at a wooden ship lying on a slant in the bay. It had three tall masts, polished pine railings and a name printed on the side: *Fortuna*.

'That's what?' I asked.

'Your new home. Archie told me.'

I looked at Mum. 'What's wrong with *King of the Sea*?' That's what our boat's called. I've lived on it with Mum all my life.

Millie pinched my cheek as she squeezed past me. 'Well, your dad can't live with you on a regular boat, can he now? Don't worry. I'll look after the place for you.'

Dad swam round to the side, staring across at *Fortuna*. 'Flipping fins! Bit different from where I've spent the last twelve years,' he said as he reached up to help Mum off the boat. Dad was in prison before we came here. He's not a criminal or anything. Well, he broke the law but it was a stupid law. He married a human. That's my mum. He's a merman. Makes it a bit difficult when she can't swim and he can't go on land, but they manage, somehow. She used to be a brilliant swimmer till she was hypnotised into being afraid of water. Neptune did that, to keep them apart. She's still nervous about it now, but Dad said he's going to teach her again.

Mum hitched up her skirt and stepped across onto the jetty. It led all the way out to the ship, bouncing and swaying on the water as we made our way along it.

I climbed aboard our new home. It was huge! At least twenty metres long with shiny brown wooden decks and maroon sails wrapped into three neat bundles. It lay perfectly still at a small tilt, lodged in the sand. It looked as if it had been waiting for us.

I stepped into the cabin in the middle of the boat and found myself in a kitchen with steps leading forward and behind. I tried the back way first. It led to a small cabin with a bed, a beanbag and a polished wooden cupboard. Circles of wavy light bounced onto the bed from portholes on either side. Definitely my bedroom!

I ran through to the other side. Mum was twirling round in a big open living room, a table on one side, a comfy-looking sofa tucked snugly into the other.

'What will we do with all this space?' she gasped. Sunny golden rays beamed into the room from skylights all along the ceiling. Ahead, a door led to another bedroom.

'What about Dad?' I asked. 'How's he going to live here?'

Before she had a chance to reply, a large trapdoor in the floor bounced open and he appeared below us. That was when I noticed there were trapdoors everywhere, leading down from each room into another one below. The ship was lodged in the seabed with a whole floor half submerged, so you could swim around in it underwater.

'You want to see the rest of your new home?' Dad's

eyes shone wide and happy.

I inched down through the trapdoor to join him. Almost as soon as I did, my legs started to tingle. Then they went numb. Finally, they disappeared altogether.

My tail had formed.

It does that when I go in water. Sometimes I'm a mermaid, sometimes I'm a girl. That's what happens when a woman and a merman have a baby.

I'd only found out recently, when I went swimming with school. Thinking about that first time made me tremble. In fact the thought of Brightport High made me feel sick, even now. I'd dreaded going there. School itself didn't bother me, only some of the people. One in particular: Mandy Rushton. Just thinking about her was enough to make my skin prickle. All those times she'd humiliated me, calling me names in front of the class, tripping me up, stealing my friends, turning them against me. I used to have nightmares about her staring at me inside a huge tank, calling me a freak. I'd wake up, cold and sweating, and then have to face her all over again in real life.

At least I'd got my own back in the end when I turned into a mermaid in the pool, right in front of her eyes. It was worth all the bullying just to see the look of stunned silence slapped across her face that day.

No it wasn't. The only thing that made the bullying worth it was knowing I would never, ever have to see her again.

Bullies like Mandy Rushton were a thing of the past.

'Bit bigger than *King of the Sea*, eh?' Dad said as I lowered myself down towards him. He took hold of my hand and we swam round the lower deck together. 'Look!' He pulled me through an archway in the centre and through purple sea fans that hung like drapes from the ceiling. Fern-like and feathery, they swayed delicately with the movement of the water. Dad squeezed my hand.

A couple of red and white fish swam in through an empty porthole, pausing to nibble gently at the side of the boat before gliding between the drapes. One of them swam up to slide along his tail. 'Glass-eyed snappers,' I said as he flicked it away. Dad smiled. He'd taught me the names of all sorts of fish on the way here.

I swam back to the trapdoor and hoisted myself up. 'Mum, it's amazing!' I said as I watched my tail form back into my legs. Mum stared. She obviously hadn't got used to it yet. She'd only seen it happen a few times.

Then Dad joined us and Mum turned to sit with her legs dangling over the trapdoor, gazing at him. He reached onto her lap to hold her hands. She didn't seem to notice the bottom of her skirt was soaking wet. Just grinned stupidly down at him while he grinned stupidly up at her.

I realised I was grinning stupidly at both of them.

Well, most people don't have to wait till they're twelve before they get to see their parents together. I never knew it would make me feel so warm, so complete.

I decided to leave them to it. They wouldn't notice if I went out to explore. They'd hardly noticed anything except each other since we set off to come here! Not that I minded. After all, I'd nearly got imprisoned myself, getting them back together. I guessed they wouldn't mind a little time on their own.

'I'm going out for a bit,' I called. 'Just for a look round.'

'OK, darling,' Mum replied dreamily.

'Be careful,' Dad added.

I nearly laughed as I climbed out of the boat. I looked out at the turquoise water and marshmallow sand. Careful? What of? What could possibly hurt me here?

I walked along the beach for a while, watching the sun glint and dance on the water in between the ships. The sand was so white! Back home, or what used to be home, in Brightport, the sand was usually a dirty beige colour. This sand was like flour. My feet melted into it as I walked. I could hardly feel the ground. A gentle breeze made the sun's warmth feel like a hairdryer on my body.

Wading into the sea, I couldn't help glancing around to check there was no one around. Just habit. I still hadn't got used to the idea that being a mermaid didn't make me a freak here, on this secret island where merfolk and humans lived together. The only place of its kind in the world, protected by the magic of the Bermuda Triangle.

There were some people up on the cliff behind me, standing in front of a cluster of white buildings. For a moment, I considered scrambling up the hill to join them. Then I looked out at the water and saw faces – and then tails. Merpeople! I had to meet them!

As my legs formed back into my tail, I wondered if there were any others on the island like me. Half human, half merperson. That would be *so* cool! Either way, at least I could live here with my mum and dad without us having to hide what we were.

Shoals of tiny fish escorted me out towards the group, gliding and weaving around me. Thin black bodies with see-through fins, they led me along through the warm water, slowing down every now and then, almost as though they were making sure I could keep up. Wavy lines rippled along the seabed like tyre tracks. A troupe of silver jacks swam past me in a line, each one silhouetted against the sand below, their shadows doubling their gang's numbers.

I flipped over onto my back, flicking my tail every now and then to propel myself lazily along, until I remembered I was meant to be looking for the merpeople.

I stopped and looked round. The island was a speck in the distance, miles away. How long had I been swimming?

The merpeople had moved on. A chill gripped my chest as I realised I was gliding over some dark rocks: hard, grey, jagged boulders with plants lining every crack. Fat grey fish with wide-open mouths and spiky backs glared at me through cold eyes. Long trails of seaweed stretched like giant snakes along the seabed, reaching upwards in a clutch of leaves and stems.

As I hovered in the water, I could feel myself being pulled along by a current. It felt like a magnet, drawing me towards it, slowly at first then getting stronger. I swam hard against it, but it was too strong. It was reeling me in like a fishing line. Blackness swirled ahead of me. Then I remembered. The Triangle.

Everything sped up, like a film on fast forward. Fish zoomed past, weeds and plants lay horizontal, stretched out towards the edge of the Triangle, the well that led to the deepest depths of the ocean.

My chest thumping, my throat closing up, I worked my arms like rotary blades, pounding through the water. My tail flicked rapidly as I fought to get away. I swam frantically. *Keep going, keep going!*

But every time I started to make progress, the current latched onto me again, dragging me back out to sea. We were locked in a battle, a tug of war between me and – and what? Fear surged through me like an electric current, powering my aching arms for one final push.

It was just enough. I was getting away. The current loosened its grip. The sea soon became shallow again, and calm, as though nothing had happened. I wasn't taking any risks, though. Catapulting myself through the water, I swam back to our bay and made it to the ship breathless. I pulled myself out and sat panting on the deck while my legs returned.

Mum poked her head out of the cabin. 'You OK, chuck?' she asked, passing me a towel.

I nodded, too out of breath to reply. I rubbed myself dry as I followed her back into the kitchen.

'Here y'are,' she said, passing me a couple of onions and a knife. 'Might as well make yourself useful.' Then she looked at me more carefully. 'Are you sure you're all right?'

Was I? That was a good question. I opened my mouth to answer her, but stopped when I heard voices coming from below deck.

'Who's that?'

'Oh, visitors, downstairs with your dad. They've been coming all afternoon.'

I gently shut the trapdoor. I couldn't face new people yet. I didn't even want Dad to hear what I had to say. I don't know why. Something to do with how happy he was, and the fact that he kept giving me all these smiley, loving looks. Well, he would do, wouldn't he? He hadn't seen me since I was a baby. And I didn't want him to know his baby wasn't quite so happy right now, or quite so sure about this new dream home of ours.

My hands shook as I started to peel the onions. 'Mum,' I said carefully.

'Mm?' she replied through a teaspoon lodged in her mouth. She says it stops your eyes watering.

'You know that stuff Archie told us on the way here, about the big well in the ocean?'

'Bu big well im be oshug?' she replied, the spoon waggling about as she spoke.

'What?'

She pulled the spoon out of her mouth. 'The big well in the ocean?' she repeated.

'The one that leads to the deepest depths of the ocean,' I added, as a shudder snaked through my body. 'I felt something just now. Pulling me out to sea.'

'Emily, you're not to go out there!' She said, grabbing my arms. 'You stay close to the island.'

The shudder jammed in my throat. 'It was really strong, Mum,' I said quietly.

'Of course it's really strong! It's protecting the whole area! You know what Archie said. Do you hear me, Emily?'

I nodded, swallowing hard. 'Yes, I hear you.'

She stared at me, holding my eyes with hers. 'I'm

not going to lose you, Emily. You promise me you'll keep away from there.'

'I promise.'

She pulled me towards her and hugged me tight. 'Good. Right,' she said. 'You silly thing, you're shaking.' She squeezed me tighter. 'Come on, it's OK. Let's get this veg done, and we'll try not to think about big wells and the deepest depths of the ocean, OK?'

'OK.' I forced a smile. 'I'll try.'

We worked in silence after that. I couldn't think of anything to say. All I could think was that it would take more than chopping a few onions to make me forget the fear I'd felt out there, clutching and snapping at me like a shark trying to drag me to the bottom of the sea.

Mermaids? Yeah, right!

You're as bad as my dad.

He reckons they're real, too. Reckons he's seen one. He says it was on his way back from The Fisherman. That's our local pub. Clear as day, he says.

'Well, that goes to show how reliable your vision is after ten pints of Guinness,' my mum says. 'You couldn't even tell it was the middle of the *night*!'

'Clear as day,' he says again. 'It's just an expression, love.'

Mum says he'll be seeing more than mermaids if he doesn't start pulling his weight. Then she has a go at me for leaving my *Girlchat* magazine lying around. Yell their heads off at each other and nag me. That's all they seem to do, nowadays.

They didn't always argue. Not this much, anyway. It's been like this ever since we heard that the council are planning to pull down our home. We live on a pier and they say it's not safe. Problem is, my parents work on the pier, too. So that's job and home gone in one swift swing of a crane. Or blast of dynamite. However they do it.

The place is a dump, anyway. I don't care what

happens. Well, maybe I do, a bit. But who cares what I think?

So today, right, Dad charges upstairs to the flat at lunchtime. He usually goes to the pub, but he says he's been somewhere else.

'Where?' Mum eyes him suspiciously.

'Look,' he says. He's got a magazine in his hand. A brochure.

Mum takes it off him. '*Mermaid Tours*?' she says. 'Oh, for Lord's sake, Jack, when will you grow up?'

'No it's not – it's not – ' he blusters. 'It's just the name of the company, Maureen. It caught my attention, that's all.' He grabs the brochure back off Mum, rifles through it as though he's looking for something in particular. 'I've been looking for something to take our minds off everything. I thought this might help.'

'There!' he says suddenly, opening it up and slamming it onto the table. Mum sits down to read it. I have a look, too. Not that I'm interested or anything. I just want to know what the fuss is about, that's all.

'A cruise, Jack?' Mum looks at him in this way she has, with her tongue in her cheek and her eyebrows raised so high they nearly disappear into her hair. 'We're on the verge of losing our livelihood and you want us to spend every last penny we haven't even GOT on some ridiculous holiday!'

Dad takes a deep breath. 'Maureen,' he says in a rumble. When he speaks again, he says each word on its own, like he's talking staccato. 'What. Kind. Of. Fool. Do. You. Take. Me. For. Exactly?'

Mum gets up from the table. 'You really don't want me to answer that, Jack.'

'Look!' Dad suddenly shouts. Dad never shouts. We both look. He's pointing at the page. 'I'll read it to you, shall I?' And before we have time to answer, he starts reading.

'Enter our EXCLUSIVE competition and you could win one of our superlative MERMAID TOURS holidays! Every month, one lucky reader will win this FANTASTIC PRIZE. Just complete the following phrase in 30 words or less: "Mermaid Tours are the best holidays around because . . . "

Remember to tell us which of our fabulous cruise holidays you'd like to go on, and post the coupon off to us. You could be our next lucky winner!'

Dad puts the magazine back on the table.

'Well,' Mum says, picking up the magazine. 'A competition. Why didn't you just say so?'

I roll my eyes at Dad. He clamps his jaw shut and doesn't say anything.

Mum and Dad are complete fanatics about competitions, especially Mum. She reckons she's got a system. It works, as well. Our home is littered with teddy bears and toasters and electronic dictionaries she's won from stupid competitions in magazines. We had three vacuum cleaners at one point. She even won a weekend break once. Not that I know much about that. She and Dad went without me. I had to stay at home with a babysitter while they went off to live it up in Paris. I still haven't properly forgiven them. Not that I should have been too surprised. I'm always bottom of the list round here.

But this. Well, I wouldn't mind a cruise holiday. Lying on a sun lounger on an enormous ship gliding through the ocean, hot sun, warm pool, all the food I can eat, non-stop sweets and no one to stop me drinking as much pop as I want. I've heard about these holidays. It's all included.

'You know how good you are at these things,' Dad says, edging closer to Mum.

'Don't try flattery, Jack,' Mum says. 'It doesn't suit you.'

But I know she'll do it; she can't resist. I catch Dad's eye. He winks and I half smile back. Well, he's still stupid believing in mermaids.

Later that day, I catch Mum leafing through the brochure. 'Look at this one,' she says. I glance over her shoulder. *Bermuda and the Caribbean. Experience the magic for yourself. Enjoy all the comfort and enchantment of our Mermaid Tours cruise. Swim with dolphins. Bask in year-round sunshine heaven.*

'That's the one, I'd say.' She nibbles the side of her mouth. 'Right, leave me alone, now. I need to think.'

She won't show either of us what she's written. Says it'll jinx it. But something changes around the place after she's sent it off. We all start talking about what we'll do on our cruise holiday and what it'll be like. Mum and Dad get on; they even smile at each other occasionally. Even more bizarrely, they lay off having a go at me. For a few days. The closing date's in a week.

But then the week's up and we don't hear anything. Another week passes, and another, and another. Nothing.

We haven't won. Mum's luck's run out, after all.

And gradually, the sniping starts again, and then the shouting at each other and getting at me every five minutes. Back to normal. And underneath it all is the looming truth that no one's saying out loud, that we're about to lose everything.

Well, why should I expect anything different? It is *my* life we're talking about here.

Oh, I haven't told you my name yet, have I?

It's Mandy. Mandy Rushton.

Chapter Two

J jumped out of bed. Shona was arriving today!
Shona's my best friend. She's a mermaid. Full
time. Not just when she goes in water, like me.
Back home – I mean, back in Brightport – I used to
sneak out at night to meet up with her. That was
before anyone knew about me being a mermaid.
Now we could see each other every day!

I couldn't believe it when she said they were
coming too. It was Neptune's idea, but I'd never met
her parents and didn't know if they'd agree to it.
Mind you, looking around me, it was hard to imagine
anyone *not* wanting to come and live here. As long as
you didn't go anywhere near the edge of the Triangle. Well, I wasn't going to think about that today.

I'd stick close to the coast, like Mum said, and everything would be all right. It all looked different this morning anyway. Nothing this beautiful could be dangerous.

Maybe if I told myself that enough times, I'd believe it.

Dad swam up to the trapdoor in the living room as I was getting some breakfast. 'There's someone here for you, little 'un,' he said. 'And look, I got you something.'

He darted away as someone else appeared below me. Someone with long blonde hair and a big smile. Shona!

I shovelled a last spoonful into my mouth and jumped down through the trapdoor with a splash. My legs melted away, turning into a tail.

'I couldn't wait to see you,' Shona said, swimming towards me to hug me tight.

I hugged her back. 'When did you get here?'

'Late last night.' She nodded towards the porthole she'd swum through. 'Althea brought me over to North Bay. She lives next door to us at Rocksea Cove. Come and meet her.'

'Here you are.' Dad swam back over, smiling broadly as he held something out to me. A doll. It had bright red spots on its cheeks, golden hair and a frilly pink tail.

'Um. Thanks, Dad.'

'You like it?' he asked, anxiously tugging at his ear.

'Sure. I'll play with it later, perhaps.'

'I wanted to give you something like this years ago. I've been saving it,' he said, his eyes going all misty and dreamy. They seemed to do that a lot. I don't know if he realised I was nearly thirteen.

Once we were outside, I grimaced at Shona and she laughed. Then I had a pang of guilt. 'Hang on,' I said. I swam back in the boat and kissed Dad on the cheek. It wasn't his fault I'd grown up without him. It wasn't his fault we hadn't worked out how to communicate with each other yet, either. It would come. It had to.

'What's that for?' he asked, lifting his hand to his cheek.

I shrugged, smiling briefly. 'See you later,' I said.

Outside the boat, a mergirl with jet black hair tied back in a ribbon was waiting in the water with Shona. The ribbon looked as if it was made out of gold seaweed. Her tail was green, with silver stars painted on the end.

Shona turned to me. 'This is Althea. She's going to show us round the island.'

'Great,' I said with a tight smile as a pang of jealousy hit me. How could I compete with a full-time, proper mermaid with stars in her tail and gold seaweed in her hair? I was going to end up without a best friend again.

'We're picking up Marina first,' Althea said.

Shona linked my arm. 'That's Althea's best friend,' she added, laughing as she read my mind. She does that sometimes. That's why she's such a brilliant best friend.

'Stay close to the coast here,' Althea warned as we set off, doubling the fear that was already starting to gnaw at my insides. 'There's quite a current round the northern end of the island.'

As if I needed to be told that! I couldn't speak. My mouth was so dry it felt like it had sand in it.

Althea pointed to the hill behind us. 'That's where a couple of the human families live,' she said, pointing up at the white buildings I'd seen the day before. 'They look after allotments for the whole island.'

For a moment I wished I'd gone up to meet them yesterday, after all. If I had, maybe I'd be looking around at everything with wide innocent eyes like Shona was doing now, instead of waiting for something awful to happen. I had to shake the feeling away. I linked Shona's arm and smiled at her. Swimming on, I made sure we stayed as close to the shore as possible.

We followed a low line of rocks that jutted out into the ocean. 'That's Barracuda Point,' Althea said.

'Why's it called that?' Shona asked.

'You'll see,' she smiled. 'Wait till we're on the other side.'

We rounded the tip and swam on a bit further before Althea stopped. 'OK, look now.'

We turned and looked back.

'Sharks alive!' Shona gasped. I stared in silence. A low line of rocks twisted out from the shore, stretching out into a long thin body. At the tip, it narrowed into a sharp point, dinted and creased along the middle, like a jaw-line filled with sharp teeth. Jagged rocks stood along the top like fins. Dark and menacing, it looked as though it could easily come to life with a snarling twist of its body. A cold shiver darted up my spine, prickling into my neck.

'It's meant to protect the island,' Althea said.

'What from?'

'Everything. There's all sorts of bogey-mers lurking, you know.'

'Really?' I asked, shivering. 'Like what?'

Althea laughed. 'It's just kids' stories. Monsters and stuff.' Then she stopped smiling. 'But there's something to them, I reckon. I've never been able to quite put my fin on it but I've always had a sense of something…something below the surface.'

'Have you ever been pulled out to sea?' I blurted out before I could stop myself.

'What?'

'By – by the current,' I faltered.

'We avoid certain spots. We learn very quickly about that.'

'And what happens if you don't?' I asked, holding my breath while I waited for her to answer.

Althea lowered her voice. 'The bogey-mer will get you!' she said. Then she looked at my face and burst out laughing. 'Come on, I'm only joking. It's kids' tales, like I said.' Then she turned suddenly, shaking her hair so it splashed onto the water, spreading golden droplets in an arc around her. 'Come on. Let's go and get Marina.'

She moved on. As we swam, Shona gave me an occasional sideways look. I smiled at her and tried to act casual but my body felt stiff and clumsy as I pushed myself through the sea.

The water soon became warm and shallow and colourless as we skirted the edges of the island. No currents, nothing weird. Althea was right. We just had to avoid certain spots and everything would be fine. I began to relax. We came to a wide bay. Swimming into it, the water turned cool and deep. Twisted rock formations stood along the edges.

'Double Arch Bay,' Althea said.

Ahead of us, two giant arches were cut deep into the rocky shore. Althea ducked under to swim through one of them. Shona went next. Then I flicked myself down and slipped through.

We swam across a small reef. Neat clusters of plants and coral were dotted about like a well-tended park. An elderly merman with shiny blue eyes and a thin grey tail swam across them, snipping at weeds with a knife made from razor-shells.

'Hi Theo,' Althea said.

He nodded at us. 'Morning, girls.'

'Theo's the gardener,' Althea explained as he swam off to tie some wilting pink plants into a bundle with seaweed.

There were archways everywhere. Some were tiny gaps in the rocks that I'd have missed if Althea hadn't pointed them out, others wide jagged holes big enough for a whale to get through.

Eventually, we came to a shimmery purple rock with a neat round hole in the middle. 'This is where Marina lives,' Althea said. She tapped a pink fish hovering at the entrance, a gold bell dangling from its tail. Immediately, it wriggled its body and a delicate sound chimed out.

A mermaid swam towards us from inside. She had curly red hair and a long gold tail with a shiny crescent moon painted on the end. 'Shona and Emily!' she said, her freckled face creasing into a smile. 'Come in while I get my things.' She grabbed Althea's hand and they went on ahead, along a narrow pathway lined with rough walls. It soon widened out into a wide living space divided up by trails of fern and kelp. An older mermaid bustled past us. She had red hair like Marina's, only hers was longer and frizzy. Her tail was bright yellow, and tapered into soft white tassels at the end.

'Don't be out all day, Marina,' she said. 'It's jellied eel soufflé tonight and we're eating early. I've got my synchro-swim class at seven.' Then she smiled at Shona and me. 'Hello girls,' she added. 'Welcome to Allpoints Island.'

Shona and I smiled back before following the others into a small space with a soft seaweed bed and drapes all round it. A huge pink sponge was squashed into one corner, a crystal mirror in another.

'My room,' Marina said.

I sat on the sponge. It squelched and bubbled under me. Shona laughed. 'It's swishy!'

Swishy – that's Shona's word for *everything* she likes. 'Squishy, more like,' I said as I tried to get up.

Althea swam towards the entrance. 'Come on,' she said. 'There's loads to show you.'

Marina grabbed a patchwork bag made of leaves and reeds and we followed Althea through the arches and back out into the bay. We swam along stretches of rocky coastline, interspersed with coves of all shapes and sizes: some wide and sandy, others tiny winding channels you could almost miss.

Everywhere we looked, spots of sunlight bounced on the water, white foamy waves washed gently over rocks, palm trees reached gently out from marshmallow sand. High on the island, some people called down to us from a woody hill. In the sea, merfolk smiled and greeted us as we passed them. A couple of young mer-children playing piggyback rides on a dolphin waved and shouted to us. We waved back. A group of mermen diving for food nodded at us on their way out to sea. A mermaid with long flowing hair streaming down her back smiled as she was pulled along by a swordfish on a lead.

It was all so different – and yet so familiar. I belonged here. The fear that had gripped me yesterday floated further away with every new sight.

Swimming on, we approached a half-hidden cave in the rocky shoreline. 'There are loads of caves on the island but we only use a couple of them,' Marina said. 'School's in one of them. The other's only for really major events like when Neptune comes. That's the Grand Caves. We can show you the other one, though, Emerald Cave. You want to see your school?'

Did I? Just the thought of school washed the smile off my face. But surely this couldn't be anything like Brightport High. No one was going to make fun of me here, or delight in making my life a misery. And it *was* a mermaid school! A mix of emotions swirled around inside me as I followed Althea into the cave.

We inched along a narrow tunnel. As it twisted and turned, it grew darker and darker. Soon we were swimming in pitch blackness.

'Feel your way along the walls,' Marina called from somewhere ahead of me. I ran my fingers along the craggy layered sides as I edged down the tunnel.

Just as my eyes were getting used to the dark, the tunnel opened out and grew lighter. We came to a fork.

'Down here.' Marina pointed along a tunnel that shimmered with green light.

It led up into a deep pool inside the cave. Above us, the ceiling stretched high and jagged. Stalactites hung all around us: enormous pillars reaching almost to the water, tiny spindles spiking down like darts. Rocks glimmered and shone purple and blue and red. Next to the pool, smooth boulders were dotted about on the gravelly ground like an abandoned game of giants' marbles.

A long scroll hung from the ceiling, pictures of

underwater life drawn all over it, a pile of different coloured reeds underneath.

A young mermaid was cleaning some hairbrushes lined up on a rocky ledge that jutted out across the water. She smiled at us as we gazed around.

'Swishy!' Shona said, swimming over to the hair-brushes. 'You have Beauty and Deportment?'

Beauty and Deportment. Shona had told me all about that. I'd be studying it with her soon. And Diving and Dance, and all the other mermaid sub-jects. No more long division!

'Of course,' Marina smiled. 'It's my favourite subject.'

'Mine, too,' Shona breathed.

Althea looked at me. 'I prefer Shipwreck Studies.'

'Althea likes going out on Geography Reef Trips,' Marina laughed. 'Anything to skive her tides tables.'

'It's beautiful,' Shona whispered as we took it all in. 'Much better than my old school.'

'And about a million light years away from mine,' I added, trying not to think too hard about Brightport High.

'There are two classes,' Althea explained. 'This one's for the older kids. There's another one for the babies.'

'Two classes?' Shona asked. 'Is that all?'

'There's only about thirty families here altogether,' Marina said. 'Mostly mer-families and a few human ones.'

'Do they mix?' I asked. I realised I was holding my

breath while I waited for the reply.

'Yes, of course,' Althea said as she started swimming back out the cave. 'But they're kind of separate, too.' She blushed. 'If you get what I mean.' She glanced quickly at my tail. I got what she meant. I was the only one. Still the odd one out.

The old fears resurfaced, hitting me like a punch in my stomach. I couldn't keep them away any longer. I'd *never* find a place where I could fit in.

'But everyone gets on brilliantly,' Marina said quickly, swimming across to touch my arm. 'And we're all really pleased you've joined us. The island's organising a party for you next week, once you've settled in.'

'We haven't had any new families here for ages,' Althea added. 'Come on, let's show you the rest of the island.'

They were organising a party, just for us? Maybe I was wrong. Maybe things would work out, after all.

We continued round the coast, Althea and Marina pointing out sights all along the way: a hole in the ground that spouted orange flames in the summer, little channels leading to a maze of caves and caverns where some of the merfolk ran craft stalls. I made a mental note to tell Dad about that. At least it could be something for us to talk about. He'd learned to make jewellery while he was in prison. Maybe he could have one of the stalls.

Swimming up the jagged east side of the island, we came to a channel leading into the rock.

'Now this is something you must see,' Althea said.

We set off in single file along the channel. The sides became steeper and higher as we swam; the water grew deeper and colder, and so dark it was almost black. A soft wind whistled through the chasm. Then nothing. No movement, no sound, the sun beating silently down. I'd never experienced such stillness.

As we wound our way along the channel, Althea and Marina kept pointing things out in our path: a fossil on the canyon wall, hairline cracks in the rocks making tiny channels that split off from the main one.

'Look.' Althea pointed ahead, to where the channel seemed to come to an end. I couldn't see anything at first, just a load of overgrown bushes and reeds lining the walls. Then I noticed what she was pointing at. A gap in the rock, through the reeds. There were pieces of driftwood attached to either side of the gap, virtually covered in plants and algae.

We parted the reeds as though they were curtains and peered through the gap in the rock. On the other side, a shimmering blue lagoon sparkled with diamond glints. The water lay virtually still; green fern hung down across gaping holes in the rock; a group of flamingos gathered at the edge, standing motionless on spindly legs, long pink necks stretched straight and high. Two pelicans flew past, their wings reaching wide as they skimmed the water's still surface.

It was like paradise. How you've always imagined paradise would look.

'Swishy!' breathed Shona.

I stared so hard my eyes watered.

Marina looked nervous. 'Come on. We need to get back.'

'But we've just got here,' I said.

'We shouldn't be here at all.'

'Why not? There's nothing to say keep out, is there?'

'It's n –'

'It's nice!' Althea burst in, nudging Marina. 'And it's naughty to go there because we're not really meant to.' She swam closer and lowered her voice. 'But *you* don't know that. You could go in and find out what it's like. I've always wanted to know.'

I stared at the lagoon.

'I'm not sure,' Shona said. 'I mean, if we're not allowed . . . '

'None of the kids are brave enough. We've been told not to go in there so many times,' Althea said. 'But you haven't. You've only been here five minutes! Who's going to tell you off?'

'She's right,' I said.

Althea smiled at me. 'Exactly,' she said.

This could be just what I needed! My chance to make sure Althea and Marina would definitely be our friends. I knew I had Shona, but I couldn't run the risk of her being my only friend. I had to make sure I was popular this time. I wasn't going to be whispered about and made fun of again. If they wanted us to do it, well, then, we would. Besides, it looked *so* tempting in there. I could almost feel it inviting me in.

Shona edged away from the reeds, her tail fluttering nervously. 'Let's think about it,' she said.

We dropped the reeds and drew back, but I couldn't get the image out of my mind. The stillness of the water, the ferns hanging down like delicate chains.

We set off in silence. All around us, nature bustled. Tiny brown lizards raced across rocks. Crabs scuttled under large stones, sneaking into the safety of their hidden homes. Above us, white birds with long sharp tails pecked at the cliff, disappearing into invisible holes in the rock. Eventually, the channel's walls widened once more and the sun warmed our necks as we arrived back at the open ocean.

When the others left us, Shona came to North Bay with me. I grabbed her before we went in the boat. 'We've *got* to go back,' I said.

'Oh Emily, I don't know,' Shona said. 'I mean, we've only just got here.'

'That's the whole point!' I said. 'Like Althea said, we're new, we don't know our way around, it would be *easy* for us to get lost. Think how impressed they'll be. Please!'

Shona half-smiled. 'It did look lovely,' she murmured. 'And I suppose we haven't really had long enough to properly understand the rules yet.'

'Not long enough at all,' I said, my tail flicking with excitement. 'We're just having a look round our new home. We're keen, we're a bit useless with directions and – whoops – we've gone wrong. *No one* will be cross with us.'

I'm the first one to the door when the postman arrives. I flick through the pile: just more bills for Mum and Dad to argue about.

But there's something else. A letter in a shimmery pink envelope. I turn it over. *Mermaid Tours*!

'Mum! Dad!'

They're at the door in seconds.

'Oh my God!' Mum says, snatching the letter from me. 'Who's going to open it?' Her hands are shaking.

'You do it, love,' Dad says. 'You wrote it.' He holds my hands. I'm shaking, too.

'It's probably just some junk mail or something,' Mum says, tearing at the envelope. 'Let's not get excited.'

She reads aloud. '"Thank you for entering our competition. We are delighted to inform you that you have won our–" Jack!' Mum drops the letter and stares at Dad.

I pick the letter up and read on. '" . . . delighted to inform you that you have won our *Bermuda and the Caribbean* cruise holiday. You and your family will spend a fortnight aboard one of our luxury ships and experience all the delights of a *Mermaid Tours* holiday. Many congratulations and have a good trip!"'

For a second, there's silence. Then Mum grabs me and screams. She pulls me into a tight squeeze. She's jumping up and down. 'We won! We won!' she yells. 'We're going on holiday! Oh my God, we won, we won!'

I jump up and down with her for a second, till I can hardly breathe. She's holding me too tight. I pull away. Mum grabs Dad round the neck and kisses him. Kisses him! I don't think she's done that for about five years.

It worked. She won us a holiday! Maybe they'll get on again and everything will be all right. For a couple of weeks, at least.

Two weeks away from this dump. Wonder if anyone will notice I'm gone. Julie might. She's kind of my best friend, not that she acts like it. She never really wanted to be my best friend. She always preferred that loser, Emily Windsnap. At least *she's* not around any more.

I wonder what happened to her and her mum? One day they were here, the next they'd gone. Took the boat and everything. Well, good riddance. All she ever did was ruin things for me and make me look stupid. She got me into trouble years ago when she told on me for cheating in the arcade. I wasn't even cheating; I was trying to help her. Trying to be nice. Taught me not to bother trying *that* again in a hurry. It never works. Best just to keep your mouth shut and not get your hopes up.

Anyway, we're out of here. We're going on a cruise!

Chapter Three

We swam side by side to begin with. Below us, occasional shoals of parrotfish and bright red snappers swept across the sandy bed. When the channel narrowed, I swam ahead, slinking along the silent passageway. The ground soon became uncluttered: clear golden sand beneath us, the sun shining down, almost directly above our heads. Two silhouetted mermaid figures gliding along below the surface, our shadows came and went, appearing briefly before suddenly growing distorted with the splash of a tail breaking the water's still surface.

We came to the curtain of reeds draped down the channel's walls and the algae-coated wooden plaques. Trying not to let Shona see my quivering hands, I parted the curtain and looked through the hole in the wall. The water sparkled and fanned out into a wide lagoon. Ferns hung down over cracks and gaps in the walls. A white tropic bird flew into a hole behind me, its long tail disappearing into the rock. Nothing else moved. Shona stared.

I turned to her. 'Ready?' My voice shook.

She broke her gaze to look at me. 'Let's just get this over with.'

I glanced around to check no one had followed us, then I squeezed through the gap and swam into the lagoon. The sun burned down, heating my neck and dancing on the water. Its light rippled below us in wavy lines across the ground.

As we slid across the stillness, the water grew colder and murkier. When the lagoon narrowed back into a channel, I couldn't see my reflection swimming along below me any more. The walls lining our trail had lost their hardness. They were like chalk. I stopped and scraped my finger down the sides; rock crumbled in my hand. The channel walls stretched upwards, cold and grey and deserted.

'Emily!' Shona was pointing at something ahead. An engraving on the wall: a perfect circle with a fountain spiralling out from the centre. It looked like a Catherine Wheel, full of energy, almost as tall as us.

'Look at *this*!' Shona had swum ahead while I stared at the engraving.

I joined her in front of some ferns loosely covering

a hole in the rock. The hole disappeared below the surface. We dived down. Under the water, it was just big enough to swim into.

'Cool!' I grinned at her. A secret tunnel reaching into the rock! 'Shona, we *have* to see what's in there.'

She frowned.

'Althea and Marina will be *so* impressed. No one else has dared do it.' And before she had a chance to argue, I'd slithered into the slimy, echoey darkness. Eventually I heard her follow behind.

The winding tunnel led us deeper and deeper into dead rock: tight, cold and claustrophobic, but gradually widening and growing brighter as we swam. Bit by bit, a growing circle of light opened up ahead of us.

We swam towards it, finally coming out into a dome-shaped space in the middle of the cave. A high ceiling rippled faintly with the water's reflection.

'I don't understand,' Shona said, looking around. 'What's that light?'

I shook my head as we swam all around the rocky edges. It seemed to be coming from under the water.

'Come on.' I dived down. 'That's our answer!' I gasped. The floor of the cave was absolutely littered with crystals and stones and gold, all shining so brightly I almost had to shield my eyes. I'd never seen jewels like these. Dazzling pink rocks with sharp white edges lay on the ground in a circle, joined together by a thin line of gold. In their centre, a bright blue stone shaped like a rocket pointed up to the surface of the water.

'What in the ocean . . . ' Shona swam round and round the display, her mouth open, her eyes huge, shining with the reflection of the blue stone.

I looked round. There was more. Once we started looking, it seemed that stones and crystals covered the entire floor of the cave, packed and tucked into gaps in the rock all around us.

'Emily, I think we need to get back.' A fat green angelfish hovered between us, startled eyes staring into ours before it spun round and disappeared into a rocky crevice. 'We've seen it now. We're not meant to be here.'

I stopped gazing around. Shona was right. 'OK,' I said. 'Let's go back.' We'd found the answer to Althea's and Marina's questions. The lagoon hid a cave filled with jewels. But why? It didn't make sense.

Shona turned immediately and started making her way back towards the tunnel. But then I noticed something on the cave's wall: a picture exactly like the engraving we'd seen earlier, only even bigger. It looked like a mosaic. As we got closer I could see it was made out of jewels: a huge golden one in the centre, oval shaped and about half as tall as me, with multicoloured strands spinning outwards from it. I put my hand out to touch it. It wobbled.

'Shona!'

'Come on.' She carried on swimming.

I pushed at the jewel. It was lodged in the rock, but only loosely. We could probably get it out. I *had* to try. There was a secret in here, I was sure of it.

'Shona!' I called again. 'Just look at this.'

She stopped swimming and turned.

'It's loose!' I pulled at it, edging my fingertips underneath to lever it up. 'Help me.'

She swam reluctantly back to me. 'I thought we were – sharks!'

'You thought we were sharks?'

Shona stared at the mosaic. 'What is it?'

'Help me get it out.'

'You're pulling my tail, aren't you? We can't go round vandalising the place!'

'We're not vandalising anything. We'll put it back. Let's just see what's behind it.' An image of Althea's and Marina's faces flickered across my mind, their eyes wide and impressed with my bravery. I might even end up being the girl everyone wanted to be friends with, instead of the weedy one who got picked on by the class bully. This cave was going to change my life, I just knew it.

Shona sighed heavily, then reluctantly dug her fingers under the jewel, and we gradually levered it bit by bit out of its hole. A moment later, we were holding it between us. We lowered it down to the ground and it plopped onto the seabed with a soft thunk, scattering a shower of sand in a swirl around us.

'Now what?' Shona stared down at it.

I swam up to the hole it had left behind and poked my head into it. Another tunnel. I grabbed Shona's arm, pointing into the blackness. 'We *have* to go down there.'

'We don't *have* to go anywhere!' Shona snapped.

'*Please*! Aren't you dying to know what's in there? Can't you feel it?' This wasn't even about Althea and Marina any more. It was more like a thirst, or a magnet pulling me.

A magnet? My throat closed up as I remembered …But it couldn't lead to the Triangle. We were in the middle of the island. There was no current here, no danger.

Shona peered into the tunnel. Her eyes sparkled against the reflection of the crystals. I could see the dilemma in them. 'We just have a quick look, see what's there, and then we go home,' she said eventually.

'Deal!'

We edged our way carefully into the hole, slithering along in the silent dark. Me first, Shona following closely behind. The tunnel grew colder as we edged deeper into the rock. The edges became craggy and sharp.

And then, without warning, it suddenly stopped. A dead end.

'Now what?' I called round to Shona.

'We go back. We've looked. There's nothing there. And I'm not exactly surprised, or disappointed. Come on.'

How could it suddenly end like that? I was *sure* it was leading somewhere. I felt around on the rock in front of me. It was different from the walls. Smoother. I inched my hands around it. Then I realised why it was different.

'Shona! It's a boulder!'

'What?'

'There's something blocking the tunnel. Look, it's different from the walls. Feel it.'

Shona squeezed forwards to touch the boulder.

I felt my way around its edges. 'There's a crack all around it.' It was almost the same shape as the crystal at the other end. 'Maybe it'll come loose.'

Shona looked at me.

'Let's just try.'

'How do I let you talk me into all these things?' she said with another sigh.

'Because you can feel it, too? Because there's something down here that's making you tingle with excitement? Because the last time we went exploring, we ended up finding my dad? Because being my friend meant you got to live on a beautiful desert island? Because –'

'OK, enough,' Shona half-frowned, half-smiled. 'Don't get your tail in a tizzy. Let's just get on with it.'

It didn't just slip out like the jewel at the other end. We pushed and pushed but nothing happened. Or nearly nothing. The boulder moved slightly, rocking backwards and forwards as though it was on a hinge, but we couldn't shift it.

'It's useless,' Shona gasped. 'We'll never get it out.'

'We need to use the rocking. Get a momentum going. Look, it's swaying. If we both push it from above, it might topple. Wait till I say. On the count of three. You ready?'

Shona nodded without looking at me.

'One.' I felt around for a good hold on the rock.

'Two.' I stretched out my tail, getting ready to flick it as hard as I could.

'Three!'

We swished and splashed and pushed, grunting and heaving.

'Now, let go!' The rock swayed away from us, and then back. 'And again.' Another shove against the rock, another slight movement. Again and again, we heaved and pushed until, finally, it started to loosen.

Then Shona stopped pushing. 'I've had enough. I'm exhausted.'

'But we're nearly there!'

'I want to go back,' she said. 'I don't want to do this.'

'What's the problem?'

'The *problem* is that we don't know what's on the other *side*!'

'Exactly! But there is something, isn't there? I can almost feel it vibrating in my body.'

'Me too. And I don't like it, Em. It doesn't feel good. I don't want to know what it is, and I want to go before this place collapses in on us.'

'It's just a boulder. It's not going to collapse!'

But Shona turned to go back.

'Just one more push.'

'You do it if you like. I'm going.'

'Fine!' I went back to the boulder. It was teetering on the edge of the hole now. I could probably push it on my own. I didn't even know why I was doing it any more. I just knew we couldn't come all this way without finding out what was down here. It might be our only chance. There was something here. I could feel it. Low vibrations hummed rhythmically through the cave. What *were* they?

Fuelled by frustration, I spun my tail as fast as I could, pushed all my weight against the rock, and heaved.

Very slowly, it teetered, swaying with the rhythm of the water before eventually toppling: a huge, smooth, oval rock slipping down and away from us, almost in slow motion. Water swirled all around. The boulder was still travelling, rolling, hurtling down through the water.

It felt like when you roll a snowball down a hill and it grows bigger and bigger. Something was building up on the other side of the tunnel, below us, below the island, deep inside the rock.

'I told you, I told you!' Shona screamed. 'It's caving in! We're going to be trapped!'

'It's OK. Look.' I tried to hold my nerve. Everything was still intact in the tunnel. It was just on the other side that the water was foaming and swirling everywhere. And there was something else: a presence. The vibrations had turned into a low rumbling, way down below. Something was down there. Something that didn't feel quite so exciting any more. What was it?

'What's *happening*?' Shona screamed.

'It's just – it's the rock falling to the bottom of the caves,' I said, much more confidently than I felt. 'It's all right. Just stay calm. It'll stop in a minute.'

The rock carried on plummeting and crashing, getting fainter and fainter. Sand and rock particles swirled around, a few of them spinning softly through the hole into the cave.

And then it stopped. No more crashing. No swirling rocks or sand, no hurtling anywhere. Complete silence.

Total silence. Kind of eerie silence.

I smiled nervously at Shona. 'See,' I said. 'Told you it'd all be OK.'

And then we heard it. The rumbling. Not a flutter of excitement in our stomachs, or a thrilling vibration that we might have imagined. This was very, very real. And it was growing. Soon, a roaring noise sliced through the caves, growling louder and louder, rumbling towards us. I couldn't move. I looked at Shona. Her lips were moving – but I couldn't hear a thing. The rumble turned into a high-pitched whine, shrieking and screaming through the hole into the tunnel. I slammed my hands over my ears.

The next thing I knew, Shona had grabbed one of my hands. She pulled it away from my head. 'We have to get OUT OF HERE!' she was yelling in my ear. 'QUICK!'

I'd forgotten how to move. My tail, my arms, everything had turned completely stiff.

'Come *on*!' Shona yanked my arm, pulling me with her. My body jack-knifed into action and we hammered through the tunnel as an explosion crashed into the water behind us.

I turned round to see the end of the tunnel crumble and dissolve. Rocks fell and bounced in the water, scattering sand and bubbles everywhere, clouds bunching and spilling across the seabed like lava.

Something was reaching out from the tunnel, feeling around. Oh God! What *was* it? A huge tube, almost as thick as the tunnel itself: slimy and dark green. One side was rubbery and shiny, then it flipped and twisted over and its underneath was grey and covered in black spots. They looked like giant warts. In between them, great thick suckers grabbed onto the wall like the suction cups on the soap holder Mum keeps in the shower, only about fifty times bigger – and a hundred times uglier.

The tube flapped and flicked about, manically batting and thwacking against the sides, reaching out further and further towards us. An icy stake of terror pinned me to the spot.

The siren noise shrieked into the cave again as the tube thing moved around in the tunnel, feeling its way along. Getting closer!

Someone was screaming and screaming.

Shona shook me. 'Emily, you have to pull yourself together!' she yelled. The screaming stopped. It had been me. She pulled me through the water. 'Just swim for your life!'

We threw ourselves along the tunnel, working our arms like windmills in a tornado. I tore brief glances behind us as we swam. The tube lashed out, extending towards us like a giant worm, ripping at the tunnel walls and doubling my panic.

Propelling myself faster than I had ever swum in my life, I flung my body through the passage until I finally made it to the open space. The rock was collapsing around us as we swam.

The thing was reaching out of the tunnel towards us! No! Its end was tapered and blood red, and covered with brown hairy strands swirling about as it felt its way around the tunnel. It slid further and further out as we dashed across the cave to the next tunnel, the one that would get us out of here.

CRASH! THWACK! Slamming against the roof of the cave, the walls, the ground, the monster worm was destroying the cave, bit by bit. We were almost within its reach. *Swim! Swim! Faster!*

As we heaved ourselves into the next tunnel, I glanced behind me again. The giant worm wasn't on its own. There were at least three others, maybe more, all searching and feeling around the cave walls, crashing through the water, reaching out towards us. Slimy, scaly tentacles. What *was* it? A giant octopus?

49

A scream burned silently in my throat. Shona had virtually disappeared. She was ahead of me but the water was murky with swirling pieces of rock and debris. *One more corner, one more corner,* I repeated to myself again and again as I ploughed down the long narrow tunnel.

I threw myself at the end of the tunnel. Nearly out! Panting and gasping, my energy was slipping away. And then a tentacle spun out, coiling itself down the tunnel. It touched me! *Arrggghhh!* Rubbery slime grazed my arm. My speed instantly tripled.

A moment later, I was out. Out of the tunnel! Back outside in the channel between the cliffs. Sunlight.

Shona was there, panting and heaving.

'It touched me! It touched me!' I screeched.

'Keep moving,' she said.

But I looked back. And this time I saw something I hadn't noticed before.

'Shona!'

'I told you, keep – '

'Look.' I pointed at the wall. How had I not seen it before? Carved into the wall. A trident. Neptune's trident!

'Keep moving,' Shona said again. But her face had turned white.

We swam on, scattering shoals of tiny yellow fish as we pounded through the creek. Back into the lagoon, and out through the hole on the other side. Turning to close the curtain of reeds, I noticed the wooden plaques again. They were covered in algae, but there was something underneath. I rubbed at the algae, brushed reeds away – and I could see it. Another trident. We'd been trespassing in Neptune's own territory! No wonder Althea and Marina didn't dare come down here. How could they set us up like this? Didn't they *know* what he was like? That his rage could create thunderstorms, or destroy islands? Destroy islands! Maybe that's what he'd do now!

What had we done?

Shona was ahead of me. I caught her up without speaking. Swimming in silence, I could hardly believe any of this had really happened. Everything was totally still and quiet. No movement at all. We stopped, listened.

'It didn't follow us,' I said lamely. 'We're safe. It's OK.'

Shona looked at me. There was something in her expression that I'd never seen before. A hardness in her eyes. 'You think, Emily?' she said. 'You really think so? '

Then she turned and swam on. She didn't say another word all the way back.

Well I don't know about you, but this is not MY idea of a luxury cruise!

Swimming pool? I don't *think* so. Non-stop food and drink? Erm, *hello*? Enormous ship? Yeah, right!

We've been conned. Our holiday of a lifetime, full of 'magic' and 'enchantment', turns out to be two weeks on an old wreck of a sailing boat with me, Mum, Dad and some old guy to drive us. Brilliant.

There's absolutely zilch to do. We've been out at sea for – well, I think it might be two days, but it's hard to tell as there is nothing to distinguish one deathly boring second from the next. I'll *never* forgive my parents for this. Especially Dad. Why did he have to see that stupid magazine?

He's the only one who's enjoying himself. Mum's spent all her time inside so far, cooking or sleeping and occasionally going green and rushing over to the side to be sick. Why I wasted my time thinking it would all be happy families I don't know. When will I learn that nothing nice *ever* happens to me?

I wish one day it would. Just once.

Even the captain has got a right gob on him most of

the time. Just stands at the wheel looking out at the sea. Not that there's anything else to look at. He hardly talks to any of us. He must be at least fifty so it's not as if I want to talk to him. But he could make a bit of effort.

Dad doesn't seem to realise that the rest of us are having the most awful holiday in the world. I wish he'd pay Mum some attention, but he's too busy running round with a fishing net, getting all excited over the stupidest things. Like now, for example. I'm lying on the deck reading a magazine – well, trying to read. It's not exactly easy while you're careering up and down and having to watch out for water splashing all over the place. Dad's on the deck next to me, leaning over the edge with a pair of binoculars. He's wearing bright yellow shorts and his back is bright red to match them.

Then he leaps up. 'Mandy, love. Come and see. Quickly!'

I put my magazine down. Maybe he's spotted the cruise that we're really meant to be on. Perhaps this was just a joke and we're on our way to start our proper holiday on a proper ship! I look out to sea. 'There's nothing there, Dad.'

'Wait. He'll do it again soon.'

Turns out he's seen a turtle. A turtle! Well, excuse, me but BIG DEAL!

I decide to go inside. It might be even more dull in there but at least Mum won't try to convince me that I'm having the time of my life.

Only, something stops me. I squeeze past the captain and I'm about to open the cabin door when I catch a glimpse of something. Not just a stupid turtle. A, well, a kind of nothingness. Just ahead of us, it's all dark. The sea looks black and shiny and the sky above it is suddenly filled with heavy clouds. Great. That's all we need now, a thunderstorm.

I look at the captain. He's taken off his cap. He rubs his eyes.

'What is it?' I join him at the wheel.

'Look!' He's pointing to a load of dials. They've got numbers on them but they're changing too fast to make any sense.

'What do they mean?'

He bends down to study the dials more closely. 'They should stay pretty much constant,' he says. 'Might just be a loose connection.'

'What about that?' I nod towards the compass. The pointer's spinning round like mad.

The captain wipes his cap across his forehead. Beads of sweat bubble down his face. 'I don't know what's going on,' he says, his voice quivering. 'It happened once before. It's – we need to get away from here!'

The boat's heading towards the darkness. And I don't know why I haven't thought of this before now, but I suddenly remember a comprehension test we did in English, about the Bermuda Triangle. It was called *The Ocean's Graveyard*, about all these ships that sailed into the Bermuda Triangle never to return.

The Bermuda Triangle. Is that where we are?

I glance across at Dad on the back deck. He's still staring through his binoculars.

'Dad.'

'Hang on, I think there might be another one in a sec.'

'Dad!'

He puts his binoculars down. 'What?'

I point ahead, at the darkness. We're getting closer and closer. It's as though we're being pulled along, towards where the water's lying motionless and black.

Dad turns round. 'Mother of . . . what's that?'

We gaze in paralysed silence as the boat slowly begins to pick up speed, gliding towards the glassy blackness.

I don't notice Mum coming out from below deck, but at some point I'm aware that she's there, too. We're slipping over to one side as we career through the water.

'We're going to drown,' Mum says suddenly. Almost calmly.

'Not if I can help it!' The captain grabs at the wheel, flinging it round as hard as he can. But it hardly makes any difference. His cheeks are purple. 'Hold on!' he yells.

We're edging closer towards the silent black water. It's pulling us sideways, drawing us in like a magnet. We're slipping further and further to the side. Bits of spray spatter the deck. The boat starts to rock.

Mum's fallen onto her knees. The captain's lurching at the wheel. I'm gripping the mast. I reach out to Mum. 'Get hold of my hand!' Spray lashes against my face as the boat leans further and further over to the side. Mum reaches out, our fingertips almost touching before she slips back across the deck.

'Maureen!' Dad lets go of his rail to reach out for Mum. He's holding her in one arm, gripping a rail with his other hand. He's got his arm round her – at last. I didn't want it to happen like this.

The captain is shouting something at us. He's spinning the wheel one way, then another. It's not making the blindest bit of difference. I can't hear what he's saying. I think I'm shouting, too. I don't even know what *I'm* saying. Seawater is everywhere. We're spinning sideways towards the strange glassiness, mast first, the bottom of the ship almost out of the water.

All is darkness, water, shouting, screaming. We're going to die! Out here in the middle of nowhere, on our own. A stupid, stupid death. I close my eyes and wait for the boat to veer into the blackness.

And it does.

Or it starts to.

We're teetering on our side when the boat suddenly jiggles and shakes. It's levelling out. What's happening? It slips and rocks a bit, there's water all over the deck and I'm soaking, but we're straightening out. We're not going to die! We're safe! Everything's going to be –

But then I see Dad's face, grey and heavy as though he's suddenly aged thirty years. He's staring at something behind me.

'Don't tell me you've seen another turtle,' I say shakily.

Then the boat lurches again and I fall to the floor. That's when I see it, rising out of the water. *What is it?*

First, huge tusks, curving upwards like giant bayonets. Below them, a long, long, olive green lumpy snout. It's taller than the ship's mast. It almost blocks out the sun. Horror seeps into my body. Huge white eyes bulging and popping out like great big fat full moons on either side, lumps all over the snout. Oh GOD!

Enormous tentacles slap the water, extending outwards and up, khaki green greasy things with suckers all the way down, waving around, splashing, making a whirlpool. We're spinning into it.

I'm trying to scream but all I can manage is a kind of dry clicking sound. We're being sucked into something, into the whirlpool, a mass of tentacles rising all around us.

And then Mum's screaming. I think maybe I am, too. One of the tentacles reaches right up into the air, then hurls itself down towards the boat, grips the mast.

I'm screaming for Mum, the boat's on its side. Where's Dad?

Water everywhere, a crashing sound, and then –

Chapter Four

Shona didn't talk to me all week. That first week in our new home. It was meant to be a fresh start, a dream come true. Instead it was the worst week of my life.

She started hanging round with Marina and Althea. I don't know how she could, after they'd tricked us like that. Maybe she thought anyone was better than me. Maybe she was right. After all, I was the idiot who had finally got to live with both of my parents and been given a new life on an island full of merpeople and glistening turquoise sea and white sandy beaches, and what did I do? It didn't bear thinking about.

And yet I couldn't think of anything else. I even forgot to be scared of starting school. I drifted through it, like everything else, in a daze. I couldn't even get excited when I learned to dive with the grace of a dolphin and brush my hair like a real mermaid and sing the wordless songs of the sirens. None of it mattered. Everything was ruined because of what I'd done, and marred by a constant fear of the consequences.

Millie and Archie came round one night. Millie stared at me all the way through dinner. 'Are you all right?' she asked as she helped herself to a huge scoop of ice cream.

Mum turned to look at me, cupping my chin in her hand. 'Are you, duck?' she asked softly. 'You have been quiet.'

'I'm fine!' I snapped. 'Why shouldn't I be?'

'Your aura's looking grey and patchy,' Millie said. 'Usually means you're fighting demons in your mind.'

Dad burst out laughing. 'Don't think my little 'un would stand a chance against demons,' he smiled. Millie glared at him.

I got up to clear some plates. Anything to get away. But just then, the boat rocked violently as a wave thrashed against the side, knocking half the dishes from the table and tripping me back into my seat.

Archie and Dad darted outside to see what had happened while I helped Mum and Millie pick up the broken crockery.

'Freak wave,' Archie said, pulling his hair behind his head as they swam back up to the trapdoor to join us again. 'Seem to have been a few of those lately. Wonder what that's about.' He seemed to look at me quizzically as he spoke. I must have imagined it. What could a freak wave have to do with me?

On Friday morning, Shona caught up with me on the way to school. For a brief second, I wondered if she wanted to make friends, but the look on her face said otherwise. Her expression was like mine when I'm faced with a plate of mushy peas, or a spider near my bed.

'Have you told anyone?' she asked, pulling me into a tiny cavern that led off from the main tunnel towards Emerald Cave.

'No! I don't know what to say. What are we going to do?'

'*WE*?' She stared at me. '*I* didn't even want to go up that stupid creek in the first place! *I* didn't want to go in the cave. *I* didn't want to knock the wall down. *I* am not going to do *anything*!'

A tear burned the corner of my eye. I'd never seen Shona like this. 'Well, what am *I* going to do, then?'

'I don't think we should say anything,' she said

more softly. 'We just forget it, OK?'

'Forget it?'

'Pretend it didn't happen. Whatever it was, it must have gone back where it came from. It didn't follow us. So we say nothing. Please?'

'But what if – '

'Em, think about it. We've only just got here. Do you want everyone to hate us before we've had the chance to make any friends?'

'Of course not. But – '

'But nothing. We leave it. Please, Emily.'

I nodded. 'OK.' A drop of water plopped down from the ceiling into the pool between us. 'You're still my best friend, aren't you?' I asked as we set off along the tunnel.

Shona didn't meet my eyes. 'Let's just act normal, OK?'

A couple of merboys were coming along the tunnel. Shona smiled at them as they caught us up, then swam ahead with them. I trailed behind, pretending to get something out of my bag.

We hadn't got much further when I noticed the water around me was swaying and swirling. It was building up, spinning round. I tried to move forward, but got thwacked against the side.

The caves were shaking. A thin stalactite fell and crashed down from the ceiling, missing me by inches. I jerked backwards through the water, scraping my back on the rock. Within seconds, merpeople were rushing from the caves.

'Quick – out!' a merboy shouted as he raced past me.

I didn't need telling twice. We pelted out through the tunnels, back to open water. Outside, others were already gathered. Someone was swimming in between them, talking to groups of people, telling them to move on. Then he turned and I saw his face. Archie!

What was going on?

I swam over to him. He hardly looked up. 'Just follow the others,' he said gravely. 'We'll meet in the Grand Caves.'

The Grand Caves? The ones Marina had told us about? But weren't they only for really special events?

I followed the others in a daze, my mind swirling and churning like the sea.

I gasped as I entered the Grand Caves. Impossible shapes hung all around us: upside-down forests, frozen bunches of arrows waiting to fall as one, long paper-thin flaps that looked like dinosaur wings. Drips from the ceiling bounced off majestic boulders and into the pool, ringing out like church bells.

Ahead of me, a stone platform jutted out over the water. On one side, thick marble-like columns reached down from the ceiling into the depths of the water, frilly edges folding around them like icing on a cake. On the other, the wall stretched up like a cliff side, stalagmites lining its surface, clumped together in chunky groups. Lanterns glowed among them, spreading shimmering lights across the pool as they shook. The walls were still trembling. Surely it wasn't safe to be inside if there was an earthquake?

I looked around for someone I knew. Shona had disappeared. Probably with Althea and Marina, I thought miserably.

In front of me, a long wooden walkway divided the clear azure pool. A few people were carefully picking their way along it. Then I spotted Mum. She was here, too, edging across the walkway with Millie.

'Mum!'

She looked up and waved briefly before grabbing the rails as the caves shook again. She pointed up to the stone benches that stretched high up on the cave's sides. I wondered if I should get out of the pool and join her, but then another mighty crash thundered through the caves, throwing me under.

Gasping, I gave myself up to the water. It wasn't as bad underwater: it was a bit like a jacuzzi. It might almost have been enjoyable if it wasn't for the fact that I didn't have a clue what was going on, my best friend wasn't speaking to me and the island seemed to be crumbling around us.

As I resurfaced, I spotted Shona with Althea and Marina. I knew it! A shot of anger speared through me. It wasn't fair! I hadn't exactly gone to that lagoon on my own. She'd done wrong just as much as I had. Nearly. I mean, it wasn't as if I'd forced her to go. And it was their suggestion in the first place! She looked up and caught my eye, just for a second. I nearly smiled. Then Althea said something to her and she turned away. She didn't look back. Traitor.

This was worse than Brightport High! At least then, I could sneak out at night to meet Shona. Now I'd lost her, and it seemed as if all three of them had turned against me. It was so unfair! I'd be better off going back to Brightport, I thought, my heart heavy, my eyes stinging with tears.

I didn't have long to dwell on it. All thoughts were catapulted out of my mind by an explosion of rocks as the caves shook even more violently. A column that looked like marble fell into the water with a mighty splash. Forests of stalagmites shuddered and trembled. I looked up to see Mum gripping the bench. Millie was holding her arm and looking serene. As serene as anyone can look when they're sitting on a bench that seems to be doubling as a seaside rodeo horse.

Where was Dad? I scanned the pools. And then I saw him. Terror on his face, he was hurtling across the pool.

'Emily!' he cried into my hair as he pulled me towards him.

I grabbed onto him while the caves crashed and crumbled all around us. It was growing louder. It sounded like thunder, cracking right over our heads, coming from everywhere.

And then something happened. Something almost familiar. I almost knew it was going to happen, almost remembered it from somewhere else.

The shaking stopped.

Just like that.

The sudden stillness was almost as much of a shock as the violent movement that had come before it, throwing people across the floor, dunking merfolk under the water. I gripped Dad so hard it must have hurt him. He held me close.

'Look!' Someone was calling out. I turned to see where everyone was looking. The caves were splitting! A crack opened up, starting from the base, shaking and creaking as it crumbled open. The whole thing would fall in on us. We'd be buried alive!

But I soon realised that nothing else was moving. Just one section of the caves was splitting open, almost like a hidden door. Almost as though it was being opened by someone. Or something.

Or Neptune.

The caves had split wide and high enough to let in a thick shaft of sunlight. I had to cover my eyes.

When I opened them, I saw him, riding into the caves, shrouded by dusty sunbeams. First the dolphins, then the chariot, gold and grand, carrying Neptune into the caves.

I should have known I'd be found out! Shona must have told, after all. She'd completely betrayed me. How could she?

The dolphins pulled Neptune into the centre of the caves before swimming back into the corners, surrounding us like bodyguards. Archie swam beside the chariot.

Pausing to wait for silence, Neptune rose in his seat, lifting his trident in the air. As he waved it above his head, the cave closed again, sealing us together to face his wrath. I knew what *that* was like. Knowing I was to face it again was almost enough to make me give up hope altogether.

Neptune looked around the caves. 'Do you KNOW why I am here?' he asked, his voice deep and grave. His question echoed over and over, *KNOW why I am here, KNOW why I, KNOW, know . . .*

No one dared answer. No one knew. Almost no one. He was here for me, I was sure of it. I tried to calm my thumping chest before Dad heard it.

'I shall ask another question,' he said, his voice ringing around the caves. 'Do you know why YOU are here?'

He looked round, narrowing his eyes. I willed myself to shrink into nothingness. Luckily his gaze passed me by.

More silence. Neptune clicked his fingers. At once, a line of seahorses appeared at the side of the caves. They gathered into a perfect formation and swam towards him. Then, hooking his golden gown in their tails, they raised it up behind him. Neptune sat down and nodded curtly, his diamond-studded tail fanning out in front of him. The seahorses instantly darted away.

'I will tell you,' Neptune said. 'You are here because of ME! Because of MY generosity. This island hasn't always been the happy little paradise you have here today. This was once a place of grave importance.'

He banged his trident on a rock. 'Archieval!'

Archie swam forwards. Then, bowing low, he kissed Neptune's tail. 'Your Majesty,' he said solemnly. I'd never seen Archie look like this. He had a gold sash running along his tail; his hair was tied back in a neat ponytail and seemed to shine with splashes of deep green against the pool's reflection.

'Tell these folk their history,' Neptune said coldly. 'It's about time they were reminded.' Then he sat back in his chariot, waving his trident at Archie to beckon him forward.

The caves went silent as we waited for Archie to speak.

He cleared his throat. 'Many years ago,' he began, 'life here was very different. The Bermuda Triangle was an important stronghold. Together with a most trusty servant of Neptune's, our bravest sirens worked well here, in the rich waters around Allpoints Island.' Archie paused. His tail flickered nervously. His cheeks had reddened a touch. 'This is where ships were brought down. They were relieved of their riches, which were returned to the rightful owner of all that passes on the oceans.'

Ships were brought down? What was he telling us?

That people had drowned here? I knew that was what sirens did, but to think of it happening right here! Was our new home one of those ships? Maybe someone had died in my bedroom!

My mind swirled with grim and gruesome images. But the images were real! All the stories Archie told us on the way here – they were all true. And what about the ones he *hadn't* told us? They were probably even worse. This place wasn't paradise at all. It was more like a setting for a horror film. I could hardly concentrate as Neptune started talking again. 'Thank you, Archieval. And then what happened?'

Archie glanced back at Neptune before clearing his throat again. 'The, er, the trusty servant I told you about. One day, he – '

'TELL THEM WHEN!' Neptune exploded.

'Almost a hundred years ago – '

'EXACTLY! NOT a hundred! Ninety-two years ago! Do you hear me? Ninety-two. That is my POINT!' As he shouted, a wave washed through the pool. I held onto Dad to steady myself.

Neptune sat back down in his chariot, his face purple with rage. He clicked his fingers and a dolphin rushed forward. Turning onto its back, it flapped its tail in front of Neptune's face like a fan. After a while, Neptune cooled down and he waved the dolphin away. He motioned to Archie once again. 'Continue.'

'Ninety-two years ago, this trusty servant went to sleep.'

Dad pulled away from me. 'You're talking in riddles, Archie.'

What was he doing? Had he forgotten how powerful Neptune was? Or that it was only thanks to him that we were here? Or how easy it would be to send him back to *prison*? He let go of me and swam towards Archie. 'Tell us what this is about. Who is the trusty servant that you keep mentioning? If you're telling us a story, tell us the whole thing.'

Archie glanced at Neptune, who shrugged disdainfully.

'All right,' Archie said. 'I'll tell you.' He took a deep breath. 'I'm talking about the kraken.'

The cave filled with sound: people whispering, talking, gasping. Merpeople turning to each other with questions on their faces and fear in their eyes.

A mergirl from my class was in front of me in the water. 'What's the kraken?' I asked in a whisper.

'It's a huge, fierce monster.' she whispered back. 'It's just a myth, though. It's not real.' She turned back to face Archie. 'Or at least that's what we've always thought.'

My body shook. My tail was spinning so vigorously the water was frothing around me.

A mermaid I didn't recognise held up her hand. She had deep wrinkles in her face and piercing blue eyes. 'Archieval, if this is true, why didn't our parents tell us about it? My great-grandparents would have been alive while it was around. Surely they would have passed this on?'

Archie glanced once more at Neptune for approval. A brief nod in reply.

'The merfolk who lived here at that time were the kraken's keepers. The kraken works for a hundred years, then sleeps for another hundred. The last time it went to sleep, one small ship somehow managed to find its way through the Triangle's border. With no kraken to bring it down, the ship ended up here.' Archie looked at the people sitting along the stone benches. 'Those folk were your ancestors,' he said.

'But we don't know anything about this,' one of the women called down. I recognised her from the ships in our bay. 'Surely someone would have told us!'

'Once the people had landed at the island, it turned out many of the merfolk were happy for them to stay. In a short time, friendships were formed. Apart from a very small number of the kraken keepers who were assigned to special duties elsewhere, most of the merfolk decided to stay here, as did most of the humans.'

'You haven't answered my question!' the woman shouted.

'Memory drug,' Archie said simply. 'They volunteered. That was their choice.'

'All of them?' the woman insisted. 'The merfolk, too?'

'We can use it on anyone,' Archie replied. 'And it will wipe out almost everything. What remains – well, you will all have heard half-tales, stories you never quite knew what to make of, myths passed on and distorted with every telling.'

Archie's words were slowly filtering into my brain. I didn't want to understand, didn't dare follow his thinking to its logical conclusion. But the memory drug, well, I knew all about that. It was what my mum had been given for twelve years, so she wouldn't remember that she was married to a merman. Fed to her in so-called treats from her so-called friend Mr Beeston. The so-called lighthouse keeper! He'd always given me the creeps. When it turned out he'd been spying on us my entire life, it all made sense. I'd half forgiven him in the end, when he helped me get my own back on Mandy Rushton. He used the memory drug on my class so no one would remember me turning into a mermaid. But he wasn't to be trusted – and nor was anyone else who went round doling out that drug!

'As you all know, Neptune is a just and kind ruler,' Archie continued, with a slight cough. 'He allowed them to live together here on the island. No one needed to know about the kraken. Not yet. And so, you are here today. Allpoints Island has existed in this way for ninety-two years.'

A mermaid with glitter in her hair and a pink tail that flickered and splashed on the water raised her hand. 'But why are you telling us this?' she asked in a timid voice. 'Why now? And who are you anyway? We hardly know you.'

Neptune rose from his chariot, motioning Archie

to move out of his way. 'Archieval works for me,' he said. 'And he has told you your history. Now let me tell you something about your present.'

He sucked in his cheeks, clenching his teeth. 'Someone,' he said, almost in a whisper, '*someone* has dared to challenge my power.' He took a breath, lifting his trident in the air. Then, in a voice that shook the caves as much as his arrival had done, he bellowed, 'Someone woke the kraken before its time!'

Darting backwards and forwards in the pool, agitated and angry, he spoke quickly. 'Eight more years. That's how long it had. That's how long it NEEDED. That's when I would have been here for it. But no! Someone couldn't wait that long. SOMEONE had to wake it early. Do you KNOW what happens when my kraken has not had the sleep it needs?'

The caves responded with silence. No one was going to attempt to answer Neptune in this kind of mood. Not that he was known for having any other kind of mood.

'I'll tell you. It wakes in a rage. Too much of a rage for even NEPTUNE to calm it. My truly loyal servant – someone has robbed me of it!'

'What will it do?' someone asked.

'The first signs are relatively small. It will lash around in its lair, creating freak waves. This is what it does while still in its cave. As far as we know, it still IS in there. But it will find its way to open seas sooner or later, and when it does, it will set out on the only path it knows.' Neptune paused as he slowly surveyed the caves. 'Destruction.'

My tail was shaking again. 'It's OK, little 'un,' Dad whispered, pulling me close. 'I'll look after you.' He knew nothing. Nothing.

'That is why I am the ONLY one who should wake the kraken. The one who wakes it is the ONLY one who – ' Neptune stopped abruptly. He smoothed back his hair, straightened his beard.

'Well. Let me just tell you this. Without my direction, it can destroy anything in its wake. Perhaps this whole island will crumble from its rage.'

The end of the island? All because of me? I tried to swallow and found I couldn't. I had to fix this!

'Oh yes,' Neptune continued. 'And you should know this: it can bring ships towards it. Apart from a few of my loyal aides, the kraken is the only creature who knows how to pierce the magic of the Bermuda Triangle. Once the kraken leaves its caves, you are no longer safe. Discovery cannot be far away. When this happens, the days of Allpoints Island are numbered.'

Neptune sucked in his breath again. 'I have not yet decided what I shall do about you all. In the meantime, I want to know WHO DID THIS! I WILL find out! It is IMPERATIVE that they come to me!'

He stared round the caves in the silence. An occasional drop of water plopped softly into the water. No! I couldn't. I *couldn't*! I *wasn't* going to get Mum and Dad thrown off the island. I wasn't going back to that awful jail. I had to think of something.

'WELL?' he bellowed.

Then someone coughed gently. There was a bustling sound up on the stone benches. Someone was getting up. Millie! What on earth was she doing?

She flung her black cape over her shoulder and stepped towards a barrier at the edge of the pool.

'Your Majesty,' she said firmly. 'I'm not one to interfere, but I may be able to help you.'

Neptune almost smiled. He looked as though he was smiling, anyway. It might just as easily have been anger twisting his face into a contorted frown. He pulled on his beard. '*Help* me?' he repeated.

'I can see things,' Millie explained. 'I don't like to boast but I *have* been told I have something of a gift. I just need your star sign.'

'My STAR SIGN?' Neptune yelled.

'Yes, you know, your horoscope, your – '

'I know what you meant! It's PISCES of course!'

'Thank you,' Millie said through tight lips. 'That anger won't do your karma any good at all,' she added in a stage whisper. Then she closed her eyes and folded her hands over her chest. 'I believe I can tell you exactly what has happened,' she said. 'I just need some quiet.'

Neptune looked as though he was about to burst, but he didn't speak. Nor did anyone else. Could she really see what had happened? Millie's cosmic ways didn't often come to much, but she did have the odd accurate moment. What if she had one now?

'I see riches of some sort,' Millie murmured. 'What is it? Gold? Let me focus.'

Gold! She was describing the cave! No! Trust Millie to have one of her flukes when I desperately needed her to come out with her usual barmy nonsense. I'd heard enough. I had to get out.

I glanced up and tried to catch Mum's eye. She was watching Millie with a look of admiration on her face. How would she look at me when she found out what I'd done? I couldn't bear to imagine it.

I edged quietly away from Dad towards the darkness at the back of the pool. I could hear Millie's voice warbling across the water. She sounded as if she was humming. Everyone was watching her. This was my only chance.

'I'm sorry,' I whispered into the darkness and slipped quietly away.

I swam frantically through the dark tunnels, not even thinking about where they were leading me. I pounded past underwater stalagmites faintly lit up with soft glowing crystals, round twists and turns and crevasses, almost gasping for the sight of the sky. I had to get out of the caves. Had to think.

Eventually, I came out into the open water. The light shocked me. Two little blueheads hovered at the cave's mouth, pecking at the rock as though giving it little kisses.

A noise behind me. Splashing. Someone was following me!

I dived down into a thin cave under the rocks, stumbling upon a group of fat hogfish who looked up at me with black eyes before scattering away to find another den.

I watched the cave's entrance. It was Dad!

I swam out from under the rock. 'What are you doing here?'

'Emily!' He swam over towards me. 'Why have you run away?'

I retreated further under the rocks. 'I've let you down. You, Mum, everyone. We'll get thrown off the island and it's all my fault. I'm so sorry.'

Dad squeezed into the crevasse with me, scattering clouds of sand as he slithered along the rock. 'No one's going to throw you off the island, little 'un. Why would they do that?'

'You don't know!' I wailed. 'You don't know what I've done.' A tear snaked down my cheek, mingling with the water. All this time! All those years without him, and now I'd found him I'd done something so stupid, so dreadful, he'd hate me forever. I'd ruined everything.

'What? What have you done?'

I bit hard on my lip, squeezing my eyes shut.

'Whatever it is, you can tell me. We'll sort it out together.'

My face was wet with tears. 'It was me!' I blurted out. '*I* woke the kraken!'

'You *what*? But how – '

'I went exploring! I knew I shouldn't have, but I did. It was in a cave. I'm so stupid! I found it. I woke it up, Dad. I've ruined everything. I'll never be able to show my face on the island again. You've only just got out of prison and now – oh Dad, I'm sorry.'

Dad stroked my face. 'Look. I don't quite understand, but it'll be OK. We'll sort it out. I'll look after you.'

I pushed his hand away. 'Dad, it *won't* be OK. Don't lie to me. I'm not a *baby*!'

He stared at me, his face red as though I'd hit him. As I held his gaze, he nodded slowly, as though he was watching me grow up in front of his eyes, catching up with who I really was, instead of who he remembered me being. 'You're right,' he said eventually. 'Of course you're not.' He turned to swim away.

'Wait.' I grabbed his arm. 'I'm sorry.'

'You know what you are?' he asked, his voice as tight as his mouth.

I shook my head, holding back fresh tears.

'You're my daughter, that's what you are. You're a Windsnap. And you know what that means?' Before I had a chance to answer, he added, 'It means we're going to sort this out.'

'I'm not going back to the meeting. I can't. Please.'

'Who said anything about going back there?'

'What, then?'

Dad stopped swimming and searched my face.

'We're going to the cave. Show me where it happened.'

'The *kraken's* cave?'

'Why not? You heard what Neptune said. It's probably still in there. Maybe we can sort this mess out, somehow. Seal it back up so it's safe again or something.'

'Dad, it was really frightening. It was the most terrifying thing ever!'

'Worse than going back to face Neptune? You stood up to him in his own court, remember.'

I dropped my head. 'I know. That was pretty frightening, too.'

'Exactly. And you did that, so you can handle this as well.'

'I suppose.'

'Come on.' He held out his hand. 'Let's see what we can do.'

'It's that way,' I said as we came to the lagoon. It looked different. The water was murky and muddier than I remembered. Sand-coloured flatfish skimmed over the seabed, moving beneath us like shifting ground.

My throat closed up. We'd reached the carving on the wall. The trident. How on earth could we have missed it last time? Maybe if we'd seen it, none of this would have happened.

It was pointless thinking like that.

We came to the Catherine Wheel, except this time when I looked at it, I realised I knew exactly what it was. The long shoots spiralling out from the round body in the centre ...

'That's it,' I said, my voice rippling like a breaking wave. 'I don't want to go any further.'

He stopped swimming. 'We need to do this, little 'un – I mean, Emily.'

'Dad, I don't mind you calling me –'

'No.' He put a finger over my lips. In charge. Strong. 'You're not a baby. You're a scale off the old tail and I couldn't be more proud of you. And we're going to sort this out, right?'

'But it's out of bounds. This was how the whole trouble started.'

'And this is how it'll end, too,' he said. 'You don't think we found ourselves at this place by the pair of us doing what we were told, do you?'

I didn't say anything.

He reached out for my hand. 'Come on. I'll go ahead, but you need to tell me where I'm going. I'll look after you.'

Eventually, I took his hand and we swam on in silence.

Everything looked familiar, until we came to an enormous gash in the rock. Maybe the size of a house.

'In there.' I held out a shaky arm. 'Except it was a tiny hole last time!'

Dad swallowed. 'Right, then. You ready?'

'I'll never be ready to go back in there.' A solitary fish flashed past me: soft green on one side, bright blue on the other, its see-through fins stretched back as it swam away from the cave. Sensible fish.

'Come on. You'll be OK. I'm right beside you.' He squeezed my hand and we edged inside, slipping back through the rock.

But it was completely different. So different that I started to wonder if we were in the wrong place. There were no thin winding channels, just huge gaping chasms all the way. We swam through them all.

And then we came to the gold. We *were* in the right place. Jewels and crystals lay scattered across the seabed. As we swam lower, the surroundings felt less familiar. Colder. And there was something else. Something very different. The deeper we got, the more we saw of them.

Bones.

Just the odd one at first, that could perhaps have passed for driftwood. Then more: clumps of them, piled up like the remains of a huge banquet. Long thin bones, twisty fat ones – and then a skull, lying on the sea floor. A dark fish slipped through an eye socket. I clapped a hand across my mouth.

'Dad!' I gripped his hand so hard I felt his knuckles crack.

'Don't look at them,' he said, his voice wobbling. 'Just stay close to me.'

We swam into every bit of the cave. Every centimetre.

'What do you see?' Dad asked as we paused in the centre of the biggest chasm.

I looked round. 'Nothing.'

'Exactly.' He turned to face me, suddenly not in charge any more. Not strong. Just scared. 'It's gone, Emily. The kraken – it's on the loose.'

How long have we been here? Couple of days? Who knows? All I know is we're stranded on a deserted scrap of an island, the boat's broken and I'm hungry.

Nuts! How long can a person live on nuts? And water from a dodgy-looking stream. Dad reckons he'll catch us some fish. And he reckons we could fix the boat if we all 'shaped up a bit'. He's acting as if he's on some kind of Boy Scouts' trip, as if this is all part of the adventure.

Mum's hardly spoken. It's best that way. If we talked more, we might end up talking about what happened. About the –

Anyway.

It's hardly even an island. I can vaguely see something that might be a proper island, out at sea. Far too far to swim. Just our luck to get stranded on this tiny speck of land instead. Two hundred paces from one side to the other. I counted yesterday. Or the day before, I don't remember. Some time when I was collecting twigs so that Dad could build us a so-called shelter. Not that I'm likely to get any sleep. It lends itself to a touch of insomnia, getting stranded on an island the size of a pair of underpants with nothing to eat, no way of getting home and no one to talk to except your parents.

Not even the captain.

That's another thing we don't talk about. I try not to think about that, either. What happened to him? Could he be . . .

Like I said, best not to think about that.

There's a splashing noise behind me.

'Mandy! Where's your mum?' It's Dad, coming out of the water with one of the nets from the boat. He's wearing purple shorts down to his knees and he's waddling onto the shore in his flippers. He's been off looking for fish. That's all he's done since we've been here. That and mess around banging and hammering on the boat. It's washed up on the tiny beach, half-filled with water and littered with shells and stones and broken bottles. Yeah, Dad. It's going to be so easy to fix.

The net's empty, as usual.

Dad pulls his mask and snorkel off. He's grinning. What on earth can he find to smile about? Doesn't he realise we're stranded and we're all going to die? Maybe he got knocked on the head when the boat went under.

He's shaking himself dry. 'Come with me. I've got something important to tell you both.'

I follow him back to the pathetic bundle of twigs that seems to have become our home. Mum's sitting on the ground leaning against a palm tree. She's not doing anything, just staring into space. Her hair's sticking out everywhere, as though she's had an electric shock. Her face is white, her eyes unfocused. She looks like a madwoman.

'Maureen, Mandy - our problems are over!' Dad announces.

I can't help it; I burst out laughing. I mean, look around you Dad – wake up and smell the coffee. Oh, sorry, I forgot. THERE ISN'T ANY COFFEE BECAUSE WE'RE MAROONED ON A STRIP OF LAND YOU COULD MISS IF YOU BLINKED, WITH NOTHING BUT NUTS, INSECTS AND A SMASHED-UP BOAT FOR COMPANY!

'Just hear me out,' Dad says. 'You're not going to believe me, but I swear, every word is true.' There's a tic beating against his red cheek. 'I *swear*,' he repeats.

Mum sighs. 'Just tell us. What ridiculous idea have you come up with now?'

'It's not an idea, Mo. Well, not exactly. It's something I've seen.'

Mum raises her head a fraction. 'What have you seen, then?'

Dad puffs out his chest and looks from one of us to the other. 'Mermaids.' I watch the lump in his throat bob up and down. 'I've seen mermaids.'

'Oh for heaven's sake, Jack!' Mum pulls herself up and shakes out her skirt. 'When are you going to act like a proper man and sort out this mess, rather than indulging your stupid fantasies?'

She starts to walk off, wiping sand off the backs off her legs. Dad grabs her arm. 'It is not a fantasy, Maureen!' he says furiously. 'I swear on every breath I've ever taken, there are mermaids! Not here, further out. I've seen them swimming, under the water. They've got tails – long, glistening, shiny tails!'

84

Their eyes are locked. It's as if they're acting out some surreal sketch and the teacher has just said 'OK, freeze, everybody!'

But there's something about what he's said, something just out of reach . . .

'Don't you understand what this means?' Dad says. His neck's bright red and bulging. He's gripping Mum's arm.

Mum stares at him. 'No, Jack. I'm afraid I don't know what it means at all. That you're cracking up, perhaps? Well, don't worry, I'm sure I won't be far behind you.' She pulls out of his grip.

'Mo, I'm *not* cracking up!' he shouts. 'You've got to believe me! We could save our home, the amusement arcade - the whole pier!' He turns to me, his eyes wild and intense. 'Mandy, you believe me, don't you?'

'I – ' Of course I don't believe him. Of *course* I don't! But there's something. Something. What is it?

Mum's shaking her head. 'You'll forgive me if I don't quite follow your logic.'

Dad holds up his net. 'We capture one! Take it back to Brightport. We can have it on show, charge admission and everything. We'll look after it, of course. Give it a good life. People will travel from all over the country to see it! From all over the world, maybe! We'll be heroes in the town, we'll pay for the pier to be renovated. Don't you see? This could solve all our problems!'

Mum sucks in her cheeks. 'Jack,' she says, 'you haven't managed to catch so much as a *goldfish* since we got here! Even if I were to believe that you have seen a mermaid – which, frankly, I don't – how in heaven do you propose to catch the thing?'

Dad pulls at his net. 'I haven't got the whole plan figured out yet, have I? I've only just *seen* them. A group of them. Swimming in the deep water. One of them had gold stars shining in her tail. There was a merman too, with long black hair and a shiny silver tail. A merman! For God's sake, Maureen!' He grips her arm again. 'I'm telling the truth! You'll see I am.'

Mum pulls away and turns to me. 'Come on, Mandy. Help me fetch some dinner. I've had enough of your father and his daydreams for one afternoon.'

I follow Mum as we pick our way through undergrowth, scavenging for crumbs like vagrants. As usual, we don't talk. But this time, it's because of the thoughts going round in my head, thoughts I'm not sure I dare share with Mum. There's definitely something familiar about what Dad said. Something niggling away in the back of my mind. I can't put my finger on it.

Maybe it's something I've seen on telly. A film about mermaids or something. I've got this picture in my mind. Someone swimming. She's got a tail and she's spinning round, smiling, grinning – at me! She's in a pool. It's not from telly. I'm sure it isn't. It feels real. It feels like a memory.

I grab a couple of nuts and shove them hard into my pocket. Mermaids! As if! I force myself to laugh.

We'd better get away from here before we *all* crack up.

Chapter Five

'**D**ad.'

He didn't reply. Just carried on staring out to sea. We'd spent half the day swimming round the coast, trying to keep out of sight, and trying to figure out what to do next. We stopped to rest at a large rocky bay on the east of the island, just a little further down from our bay.

I swam over to join him next to a huge boulder at the edge of the bay. 'Dad,' I said again.

'I'm thinking, love,' he said without turning round. 'Just give me a minute.'

I counted to ten. 'What are we going to do?'

He shook his head. 'I don't know, Em. I just don't know.'

I looked out to sea with him. The water lapped gently into the cove behind us. Daylight was starting to fade.

I stared out at the horizon. So much ocean, stretching out for miles and miles and miles, forever, it seemed. Nothing but water. And the monster. Somewhere. A cold shiver rattled through my body. The water lay still, but how long till it would seethe with the kraken's rage? The stillness was almost worse than that, knowing it was out there, waiting.

Something flickered on the horizon. A brief flash of light. I jerked upright and peered so hard my eyes watered. There it was again.

'*Dad!*'

'Emily, will you leave me alone! I've told you, give me five minutes. I need to think.'

I shook his arm. 'Look!' I pointed out to the horizon.

Dad followed the line of my finger. 'Mothering mussels,' he breathed, squinting into the distance. His words came out like a whistle. 'What's that doing there?'

'What is it?'

'Look, red, then green.' Dad turned to me. 'It's a ship, Emily.'

A ship had got in! The kraken had already pierced the Triangle's border.

'It's not coming any closer, is it?' I asked with a gulp.

'Doesn't look like it. Doesn't mean it won't,

though.' Dad pushed off from the rock and started to swim away. 'Come on.'

'Where are we going?'

'We'll have to say something.'

'Say something?' My words jammed up my throat. I swallowed hard. 'Who to?'

'I don't know. Archie, I guess.' Dad took hold of my hand. 'Emily, there's a ship coming towards the island. The others need to know that the kraken's got out.'

'No!'

'Em, love, the monster could attack that ship. Or the ship could discover us here. That'll be the end of us all. You heard what Neptune said. We can't stay here if the secret gets out. Can't you just see it? Hordes of tourists swarming the place? They'll turn us into a zoo or something.' He turned to swim away.

A zoo. My old fears of discovery resurfaced in a wave of anguish. What had I *done*?

'There must be something we can do,' I said, swimming hard to keep up.

'This is the only thing.' Dad's voice was firm.

He didn't speak again. The water soon grew warmer as we reached the shallow sand, rippling like tyre tracks across the sea floor.

Dad wouldn't look at me. 'You go along home. Mum'll be worried.'

'What about you?'

'I'm going to see if I can find Archie.'

I didn't move.

'It'll be all right,' he said with a tight smile. Then he turned and swam towards the end of the bay, taking my last shreds of hope with him.

Mum threw her arms round me the second I arrived back at *Fortuna*. 'Emily! I've been worried sick. Where've you been?'

'With Dad. I felt claustrophobic in the caves and we – we went exploring.' My cheeks burned. I hate lying to Mum.

'Mary P, you really should listen to me. I told you she was safe,' Millie said, pouring some herbal tea from a pot and settling down on the big sofa.

'Millie saw a ship,' Mum said.

'She *saw* it?' I burst out.

Mum looked at me quizzically. 'When she did Neptune's reading. She had a vision of a ship. What ship did you think I meant?'

'Oh. No. Nothing. Yes, that's what I thought you meant,' I blustered. Great move, Emily. Just give the game away to *everyone*. 'I thought you'd said something about gold.' I tried to keep my voice even.

'Yes, well, you can't be expected to get everything right, all the time,' Millie replied, sniffing as she picked up a magazine.

'So what did Neptune say about the vision?' I

asked, holding my breath.

Millie flicked the pages. 'Not everyone appreciates my gift.'

'He told her he'd throw her off the island if she wasted any more of his time with her hocus pocus,' said Mum, smiling.

How could she smile? I could hardly *speak*. I had to get away from here. 'I'm going to my room,' I said. Before they had a chance to argue, I'd gone through to the back of the ship and closed my door behind me. Shaking, I sat down on the bed and looked round. Like all the others, the room had a trapdoor that led to the floor below, to the sea. I'd hardly used it yet. The one in the living room was open all the time and it was bigger.

I crept over to the trapdoor next to my bed and opened it up. Maybe ...

'Emily.' Mum was at my door.

I jumped away from the trapdoor. 'I was just looking at the fish,' I said quickly.

'Are you all right, love?' Mum stepped into the room and came over to me. She lifted a strand of hair off my face, stroking it behind my ear. 'If there's anything you want to talk about ... '

'There isn't,' I said, trying to make myself smile. I expect I looked a bit like a scared rabbit with a twitch. 'I'm fine, honestly,' I said. 'Just a bit tired.' I stretched my mouth into a yawn. 'Look, see. I think I'll have a lie down.'

Mum stared at me quizzically for a moment before

shrugging. 'Well, we'll be next door if you need anything.' She kissed my forehead and left.

I waited five minutes. She didn't come back. Right, this was it. I knew what I was going to do.

I eased myself through the hole. Then, dangling over the side, I lowered myself down as gently as I could, and let go. I dropped down below with a splash. Had they heard? I held my breath and waited. Nothing.

I waited a bit longer, to make sure my tail had fully formed. When the tingling and numbness had completely gone, I ducked under, swam through the big open porthole, and headed towards the ship.

It was almost like the old days: swimming out to sea under a sky gradually filling up with stars. A stripy butterflyfish raced along beside me before slipping away into the darkness, disappearing under a rock. Shoals of silver bar jacks hovered nearby, shining like pins in the darkness. Purple fans waved with the current, caressing me as I sailed over them.

It was nothing like the old days.

In the old days, I was swimming out to meet my best friend; now I didn't even know if I still *had* one. My chest hurt as I pushed myself to swim harder, swim away from the painful thoughts. The water grew colder and darker. I picked my way out towards the ship, praying there was no current round this side of the island.

After a while, I stopped to scan the horizon. Two dim lights, facing me. It was a long way out, but definitely inside the Triangle. I couldn't even see the island any more. Just blackness, except – what was that? Something flashed through the water. A boat? I held my breath while I watched. Nothing. It must have just been the moon's reflection.

I swam on towards the ship. Maybe I could stop it from finding us, get it away from the island. I had to buy some time.

Eventually, I was close enough to study it: a cruise liner with three levels of portholes and balconies, all lit up with lamps. The sides rose steeply out of the water.

I swam all around it, looking for a way in. There was a rope ladder hanging down at the back. I tried to make a grab for it but missed by inches. I heaved and jumped up in the water. No good – it was just out of reach.

I swam round again, looking for something else. And right at the front, I found it. The anchor!

Gripping the chains, I pulled myself out of the water. My tail dangled and flapped in the sea. Panting and gritting my teeth, I managed to inch my way up. Eventually, I'd done it. I clung onto the chain like a koala, my body clear of the water. Within moments, I got that tingly sensation I knew so well. My legs had come back.

I hooked my feet into the loops, then slowly and carefully climbed up to the ship's deck.

Hauling myself over the metal rail, I landed heavily on the deck. A quick look around. No one. Just me and the darkness and a row of deck-chairs. I dried myself on a towel someone had left on one of them and pulled on the shorts I'd brought with me. Then I went to look for some signs of life.

It didn't take long.

Halfway down the side of the ship, I found some stairs and a door that led inside. There were sounds, somewhere near. I followed the noise, almost sniffing my way towards it. Music. Laughter.

Soon I came out of the narrow corridor into an open space with a few people dotted about. I tried to saunter in casually, as though I belonged there, even though I knew I'd be sussed out in a second.

But I wasn't. Some kids were playing in a tiny arcade on one side; on the other, a couple of men were drinking at a small bar. A man and woman behind the bar laughed together. No one even looked up.

A flight of stairs led up towards where the real noise was coming from. *OK, you can do it.* I took a deep breath, twirled my hair a few times, nibbled on my thumbnails – and went upstairs.

It wasn't till I saw all the food that I realised I was starving! I'd hardly eaten all day.

I grabbed a paper plate and joined the queue behind a girl who looked about my age. Maybe she'd know something.

'It's great, this holiday, isn't it?' I said as we shuffled along the food table, shoving tiny sausages and crackers and crisps onto our plates.

'Mm,' the girl replied through a pizza slice.

'Wonder how long before we move off,' I said casually.

She swallowed the pizza slice. 'My mum says we're not even meant to be here. She reckons we've gone off course. Doesn't matter though, if we see it.'

See it?

'Yeah, that's what I thought,' I said, trying to stay calm. I popped a mini sausage into my mouth. 'So has anyone seen it yet?'

The girl put her plate down. 'Don't you know?'

'Oh, I'd, um – I forgot. Remind me?'

'That's why we're here! Mum says more than half the passengers cancelled at the last minute. That's how we got our places. I bet Carefree Cruises are totally fed up with that captain!'

What was she on about?

'Yeah, I bet,' I said seriously. 'What did he do again?' I asked, quickly turning away to grab another handful of crisps.

'How can you not know? He saw Triggy of course! First sighting in absolutely YEARS!'

A crisp got stuck halfway down my throat. 'Triggy?' I asked, swallowing hard.

'Don't tell me you haven't heard of Triggy.'

I tried a lighthearted shrug and a frown.

'Triggy! The Triangle Monster! I've always believed in it. Mum said it was just a silly fairy tale, but now she's not so sure. I hope we see it, don't you?'

I couldn't reply. I couldn't do anything. I tried. I opened my mouth, even moved my lips a little, I think. But nothing came out. *Triggy?* It sounded like a cartoon character. She had no idea! I thought of the slimy tentacles racing down the tunnel towards me, the suckers all along it, grabbing at the walls, the way it extended out, the hairy tapered end touching me.

The bones.

Now these people were hunting it down. Which either meant it wouldn't be long before they found us – or they'd be its next victims.

'I – I've got to go now,' I said eventually. I staggered away from the food table.

'See you in the morning,' she called before going back to her friend.

'Yeah.' *Whatever.*

I stumbled back down the stairs. At the bottom, I took a turning which I thought led back to the corridor I'd come down earlier. But I emerged into another open space. I was about to turn back when I noticed a shop, just ahead of me. It was closed now, but there was a poster in the window. I went over to take a closer look.

It was the front page of a newspaper: *The Newlando Times.*

'BRAVE CAPTAIN TELLS OF HORROR AT SEA' the headline screamed across the top of the page. I read on.

The old myth of Triggy the Triangle Monster rose up again today when Captain Jimmy Olsthwaite was rescued from stormy seas by a local fisherman.

Captain Olsthwaite lost his boat when it was attacked by what he described as 'a monster beyond imagining. The size of a dinosaur! And a dozen tentacles that wrapped round the boat like a helter skelter!'

His story has horrified and delighted tourists in equal measure.

Katie Hartnett was among those setting sail today with Carefree Cruises. 'It's so exciting,' she told *The Newlando Times*. 'My parents used to tell me stories about The Triangle Monster when I was little – but we never thought it might exist for real!'

Others have cancelled in droves. Pensioner Harold Winters was among them. 'We wanted a peaceful trip, not the fright of our lives,' he said.

The captain's sighting has not been confirmed. Coastguards are warning that it could be a case of delirium brought on by his traumatic capsize and rescue.

Three others were believed to be on board the boat with the captain. Neither they nor the boat have yet been recovered.

The boat was owned by a company called *Mermaid Tours*.

I stumbled away from the shop. I was in one of those nightmares where you're stuck somewhere, trying every exit, but there's no way out and every step takes you deeper into the horror.

I found myself out on the deck again. Leaning over the railing, my stomach heaved. My mouth tasted like iron. I looked down at the sea, deep navy in the darkness. Little bright flecks sparkled white as the water lapped and splashed against the ship. There was another boat down there. I could just make out its shape. A small yacht. It looked as if it was coming towards us. Maybe they were checking their lifeboats were working or something. Well, they'd be needing them soon, unless I could come up with a miracle.

I had to do something! I couldn't just stand here staring at the sea.

Then it came to me.

I ran up steps, down ladders, along corridors, banged on doors, called through open windows: 'TRIGGY! THE MONSTER!'

People emerged from their rooms. Dressing gowns were pulled round bare bellies and boxer shorts, women came out of their cabins in silk nighties, kids in twisted-up pyjamas.

'*Triggy*!' I shouted at everyone I saw. 'The monster! I've seen it!'

'Where?' Open-mouthed gasps.

'Over there!' I pointed – away from the island. I pointed and pointed. 'Tell everyone. Tell the crew!' I ran on as everyone I spoke to gathered along one side of the boat: all gazing out to sea, desperate for a sighting of something I wished with all my heart I would never see again.

I had to find the captain.

I ran on, down more corridors – until I barged slap bang into someone.

'Hey, what's all this?' It was a woman with a uniform on. She grabbed hold of my elbows, holding me at arms' length.

'I need to find the captain,' I gasped. 'I've seen the monster!'

The woman frowned. 'Yes, dear. I'm sure you have. Now come on, why don't you – '

'I have!' I burst out. 'I can prove it. It's – it's – ' I gulped. The memory of it took my breath out of me for a second. I started again. 'It's enormous, and it's got tentacles.'

'We've all seen the papers, sweetheart,' the woman said, smiling. 'Now, if you want an excuse to visit the captain, you can just say so. He's always happy for you kids to have a quick look round the cabin.'

Bingo! 'OK!'

The woman gently shook her head as she pointed towards some stairs. 'It's up there. Turn right at the top, straight on to the end and it's through the door ahead of you. But knock first. He doesn't take kindly to being barged in on.'

'Thanks!' I took the stairs three at a time.

I bashed on the door. *Come on, come on!*

No one answered. Come *on!* No time for politeness. I tried the door. It swung open.

'I need to talk to the captain,' I said breathlessly as I burst into the room.

Two men were sitting in front of a load of dials drinking coffee. One of them swivelled round. 'Now hang on. What's the – '

'Are you the captain?'

'I certainly am,' he said, 'and you can't just – '

'I've seen the sea monster!'

The captain leaned forward in his seat. 'The sea monster?'

I nodded.

His face relaxed into a slight smile. 'Now listen, you want me to tell you something about this sea monster?' he asked. I swallowed, and nodded again.

He lowered his voice. 'It doesn't exist.'

I held his eyes. 'It does! I've seen it.'

The captain leaned back in his seat. 'Right, let's have it, then. Big thing with tentacles, was it?'

'Yes! That's exactly what it was!'

'Right.' He was smiling, laughing at me. I had to convince him.

'It's – it's enormous!'

'Mm hm. Anything else?' the captain asked in a bored voice.

'The tentacles – they're tapered at the end.'

He turned back to his tea. I racked my brain. *What else – what else?*

'And hairy! And they've got huge great suckers all along them!' I blurted.

The captain put his cup down. 'They what?' he asked, his face suddenly hard, and focused on mine.

'And they're – they're green, and grey underneath, and warty.' My voice trailed away as I remembered the sight of it. My teeth chattered.

The captain turned to the other man. 'That's exactly what my friend at the coastguard said.'

'Sir, the newspaper report – '

The captain shook his head. 'Those things weren't in there. Come on, man. Face the facts. You saw the dials. You know we've been stuck here, spinning on the spot like a Mini in a mudbath. There's something going on and it's time we faced up to it.'

He moved his chair closer to mine and leaned towards me. 'Right, then,' he said. 'You'd better tell me exactly where you saw the sea monster.'

I'd done it! The ship had changed direction and we were heading directly away from the island.

I sneaked along the empty deck. Every single person on the ship must have been crowded on the other side, peering into the darkness for a sight of something they thought would make their holiday. I thought of its flailing tentacles, the floor littered with bones, and I shivered. If only they knew. I hoped for their sake that they never would.

I had to get back to the island. Maybe I could confess, after all. If I told Neptune what I'd done here, how I'd stopped a whole cruise ship full of people from discovering us, he might even forgive me.

I checked round one final time to make sure no one could see me. Then I slipped back into the water.

Moments later, the familiar warm feeling spread through my legs as they turned back into my tail. It shone bright in the moonlight.

Fish around me seemed to be dancing. I could make out their shapes in the darkness. They must have been happy for me. Maybe it was a sign. It was all going to be all right. I swam along, lost in my hopes that I could somehow make up for everything that had happened over the last couple of weeks. Perhaps Shona and I would be best friends again and the island would be safe. The kraken might even go away and our lives in our new home could really start.

'EMILY!'

I started and looked back, twisting round in the

water. Two people were leaning out over a balcony, waving frantically. Why weren't they round the other side with everyone else? I edged back towards the boat.

That's when I saw who it was. Mum! Thin and wiry with wild hair, waving her arms about. Someone was with her. Larger than life in a black cape. Millie! What the heck were –

'Emily!' Mum screamed again.

I swam closer to the ship but it was picking up speed. I could hardly keep up.

'Watch the propellers!' Mum screeched. 'Don't come too close!'

Millie had sunk into a deckchair next to her, her head in her hands. A small yacht was moored on a buoy, near where the ship had been only moments ago. The one I'd seen coming towards us. I recognised it now: it was our old boat! They'd followed me!

'Mum! What are you doing there?'

'We came to find you but you'd just jumped off! It was Millie's idea. The vision, the boat. She'd seen you on it.'

'What? You never told me that.'

Millie got up and stumbled across to clutch onto the railing. 'I kept it to myself,' she wailed. 'I thought it would have sounded crazy. I've heard what people say about me.' She leaned out over the railing. 'I'm sorry, Emily. I was too busy worrying about my reputation.'

'We didn't think they'd get going again tonight.' Mum called.

Oh no. My fault again. I'd made things worse *again*. The ship was only on the move because of me. And now it was moving faster and faster away – and taking my mum with it!

'Mum!' I tried to keep up. She was shouting something but I couldn't hear her any more. I could hardly even see her as the ship picked up speed.

'MUM!' I yelled again, uselessly, into the darkness.

As the ship slipped away, I let the current carry me along. No energy left. I drifted away from the ship, from the island, from everything that mattered. Tears streamed down my face as I howled in the darkness.

And then –

Noise.

Clattering – shuffling. What was happening? I mopped my cheeks with my palms.

I'd got caught in – what? Seaweed? I flapped and scratched at it. *Please not the monster.* I looked around me.

A net! I was trapped in a net! A man was holding it, pulling at a piece of rope, dragging me through the water, propelling himself along with flippers.

Flapping my tail, I tried to push myself away, but he was too strong. I struggled and fought, biting at the net, pulling at it with my fingers, cutting my hands, scraping myself all over. It was like wire. There was no way I could get through it. I scratched and screamed as he drew me through the sea.

Soon the water grew warmer and shallower. We were at a tiny island: a little sandy bay with a few palm trees, a small boat moored to a pole and a makeshift lantern propped on the beach. The man tied my net to the pole.

He pushed his mask and snorkel onto the top of his head. I couldn't make out his face properly in the shadowy light. 'I'm not going to hurt you,' he said, panting from swimming so hard. 'Trust me.'

I didn't say anything.

'Do – you – speak – English?' he asked in a very loud voice. I ignored him.

'Stay here,' he said, as though I had a choice. He disappeared up the beach as I scraped and scratched at the net, trying to get out. Moments later, he was back with someone.

'Dad, you are completely obsessed,' a girl's voice was saying. 'It's the middle of the night!' The voice sounded familiar. But it couldn't be.

'I said, didn't I?' the man replied as they came closer. 'I told you – I TOLD you! *Now* do you believe me?' He pointed in my direction. The other person waded towards me and peered at me in the darkness. As she came closer, I could just make out her face from the lantern's light.

It was –

It was –

I gasped and jerked backwards against the net, my mouth stupidly open. It couldn't be! How – ?

It was someone I knew. Someone I knew well. Someone I'd thought I would never *ever* have to see again.

Dad's caught a fish at last.

Hallelujah.

He's screaming and yelling at me to come and see it. You'd think no one had ever caught a fish in the sea before.

But it's not a fish. He's got someone with him.

'I told you! I told you!' he's yelling. 'I said I'd catch a mermaid, didn't I? Do you believe me now?'

I get closer, and I notice a tail. No! It can't be!

He has! He's actually caught a mermaid!

It turns round. I see its face, its mousy hair, skinny runty little arms. It *can't* be! It's impossible! But it is. It is. I grab the lamp and bring it closer as I stare at her.

It's Emily Windsnap!

And then I remember. I remember everything! The pool, the swimming lessons. She came to us once before she left, showing off as usual. She had a tail! She swam in front of us all, swirling it round. Grinning at me as if to say she'd won. It wasn't enough for her that everyone thought she was *so* wonderful. Julie, the swimming instructor – they all liked her more than they liked me, all thought she was better than me. She had to rub it in, didn't she? Had to prove they were right.

How could I have forgotten?

There was something afterwards – they gave us cakes. That was when it all faded. The cakes! Had they drugged them or something? And what the heck is she doing *here*?

Our eyes meet. She's as shocked as I am.

'Mandy!' she says.

I pull myself together quickly. 'Oh, hi Emily,' I say, nice and calm. I sniff and turn to Dad. 'Why are you collecting garbage, Dad?'

Dad pulls off his mask and snorkel. 'What are you on about, Mandy? It's a mermaid!'

'Dad, have you actually looked at her face?'

He gawps at me for a second before turning to Emily, and then back to me. I can almost see the realisation crawling into his mind. He points at Emily. 'But that's, that looks like – '

'Yeah, Dad,' I say, trying to sound bored, or at least as if I've got a *clue* what's going on here, 'it's Emily Windsnap.'

'But how . . . but she's a . . . ' His voice trails away. He looks at her again, then at me. 'Don't be stupid, Mandy,' he says suddenly. 'Of course it's not Emily Windsnap. It just looks a bit like her. This is a mermaid!'

Mum's on the beach. 'What's the fuss, Jack?'

Dad runs towards her, ignoring me, and ignoring reality it seems. 'No time now, Maureen,' he says. 'We need to get ready. Where's all our stuff?'

'What stuff?'

'Everything. Everything we need. Get it in the boat. We're off as soon as it's light.'

'Off?' I follow Dad out of the water. 'What d'you mean "off"? Where are we going?'

Dad stops and turns back to me. 'We're going home, Mandy. With our mermaid. We're going to save the pier. Just like I said.'

He runs over towards the boat.

'But it's broken!' I say, following after him. 'We capsized, remember.'

'I've been working day and night on this boat,' he calls back. 'I think she's ready to sail again. Pack your things, and then get some more sleep. First light of dawn and we're away.'

'Mum?'

Her eyes are vacant. She looks as if she's already given up hope. 'I haven't got a clue what's going on,' she says. 'What's that he's got in the net?'

I leave her to find out for herself as I follow Dad to the boat. Maybe we can sort everything out. Maybe he's right. It's worth a try I suppose. Anything's better than rotting on this stupid island for the rest of our lives. Even if it does mean sailing home with *fish girl*.

The boat seems to be just about holding up. It would be better if Dad had the slightest idea how to drive it. We're buffeting about all over the place. He keeps yelling things at Mum, like 'Get over onto starboard!' and 'We need to tack! Watch the boom! Lee oh!"

She yells things back but her words are washed away

by the wind and the sea water spraying us on the back deck. Just as well. Judging by her expression, it's probably best if neither of us can hear what she's actually saying.

Anyway, I'm busy with Emily. I've got to keep an eye on the net, make sure it doesn't come loose. Can't have her escaping.

'Comfy down there, are you?' I call down to her. She's being pulled along like a water-skier. She should be grateful for the free ride. 'Enjoying your little trip?'

'What are you going to do with me?' she whimpers. She's scared. Good.

'Oh, didn't Dad tell you? We're taking you back to Brightport.'

The boat swerves and surges so I don't hear her reply. Just a kind of yelp from inside the net. It could almost make me feel sorry for her.

As if!

'Yeah, we're going to put you on display,' I continue when she bobs up above the surface again, her hair plastered across her face with sea water. I smile down at her. 'Hey, maybe all your old school friends will come and visit. That'd be nice for you, wouldn't it? We were thinking maybe five pounds a visit. What d'you think?'

'What about my mum? She's stranded on a ship! I've got to find her! And my dad? Let me at least get a message to him!'

'Yeah, right!'

'Mandy, I need you!' Dad's calling.

'Back soon,' I call down to her. 'Don't go anywhere

109

now. Oh, sorry, I forgot. You can't!'

I stand up to see what Dad wants. But I don't need to ask. The boat has levelled out; all is calm. But just ahead of us is something I'd almost forgotten about.

The darkness, spreading like an oil slick in the pale morning light, pulling us in.

'Dad, what are we going to do?'

He shakes his head. 'I haven't got a clue, love. We've got to get across it, somehow.'

Mum's inching along the side deck to join us. 'Jack, are you mad? Have you forgotten what happened last time? The last fortnight foraging for food like beggars after near enough drowning? And that *poor* captain. *Have* you?'

'What choice do we have, Maureen?'

'We can think about our choices as soon as you've got us away from here. But I, for one, am not going to gamble with my life when the odds look like that!' She points to the sheet of water, glistening like glass ahead of us.

'Well, *I*, for one, am not going to live on nuts and berries for the rest of my life!' Dad yells. 'And I'm not going to go back and watch my home and my livelihood demolished either.'

'So you'll kill us all then, will you?' Mum screams.

'Mum! Dad!' I try to get between them, but the boat suddenly lurches and I slip across the deck. We're starting to tilt. We're being drawn towards it again.

Neither of them is listening anyway. They'd rather scream at each other than try and work out what to do.

'DAD!' I yell, clutching the railings as the boat dips further. I nearly fall over the side. Emily is down below in her stupid net. We're going to capsize again. I'm going to drown out here, all because of *her*. I can't believe it!

The boat lurches again.

'I can help.' A voice from down below.

'What?'

'I'll help you.'

I grab the railing as the boat leans over. Spray hits us on all sides as we skid through the water, soaking me. She looks up at me pitifully, her big brown eyes round and shiny. I turn away. I bet she's only putting it on anyway. 'And why would you do that?' I ask.

'I don't want you to die,' she says.

'I'm meant to believe that, am I?'

'I've got enough on my conscience,' she calls up. 'I don't need that as well. You can keep me in the net. Just let the rope out. I'll pull you away.'

I glance over at Mum and Dad. They're not screaming at each other any more. Mum's trying to make her way over to me. She's not even holding onto anything.

'Mum! Stay where you are!'

'Let the rope out!' Emily yells. 'Do you want to be killed?'

I glance at the rope. It's looped round and round over a hook. 'Don't try and do anything clever, right?'

'Just do it!' she shouts. 'It'll be too late in a second.'

I lurch over to the back of the boat. One last glance at the water ahead of us, then I unhook the rope. 'I'm warning you,' I shout as I throw it into the water.

The coil lands with a splash. Then nothing. Where's she gone? She's disappeared! I scan the surface of the water. Where is she? She must be in there somewhere.

I'm staring so hard at the water it looks like it's changing colour, getting darker. It *is* changing colour! There's a shape in there! A huge grey outline of something – something very, very big.

Without warning, it bursts through the surface. A piercing, screaming siren sound screeches into the sky as an olive green tentacle rises up, way up above us, then sears downwards to wrap itself over the top of the boat like an arch.

No!

'Mandy!' Emily's yelling. Where is she? Did she know it was here? Did she make this happen?

The monster lifts the boat right out of the water, high up into the air. I can see the underside of its tentacle. It looks like a giant worm, extending and retracting, slithery and lumpy. Gasping and retching, I fall against the railing, clutching on for my life.

With an almighty crash, it drops us back down onto the water, exploding against the surface.

We're such fools! How could we let it happen *again*? *She's* done this to us. She's made it happen. She tricked us, somehow.

The thing has tentacles all over us, sliming over the boat, roaming, searching for things to grab and lurch onto. I'm slipping across the deck, water everywhere. It sucks the boat down, throws it around, tosses us one way and then another.

Any second now, we'll all be in the water. Should I pray?

As if praying would help.

The only thing giving me courage as the boat is thrown over, as I clutch the railings, hold my breath, grab the lifebelt, is one single thought:

I'll get you for this, fish girl. I will SO get you for this.

Chapter Six

*T*otal stillness. Utter darkness.

What had happened? Where was I?

I rubbed my eyes, tried to move. I was still inside the net, trapped under a rock. Out of the darkness, a shape was coming towards me. It looked like a submarine, gliding along the very bottom of the sea, black on top, white underneath, large fins flapping below. As it came closer, it opened its jaw. Serrated lines of teeth, above and below: the sharpest bread knives.

A killer whale!

I grabbed the net, rubbing it hard on the edge of the rock, sawing and scraping frantically. My fingers bleeding and raw, I yanked and tugged at the net. *Come on, come on! Break!*

The string started to fray and tear. I was nearly out.

But then the water was swirling all around me, whisking up and round, faster and faster like a whirlpool.

It was back.

The sea filled with giant tentacles, writhing and grasping and sucking. I crouched tight under the rock and prayed it wouldn't see me.

THWACK! They crashed against a rock, only metres away from me. It split and crumbled instantly. My tail flapped wildly; my teeth rattled so hard my jaw hurt.

CRASH! The tentacles came down again, scattering a spiralling shoal of barracuda before searching around for their next target.

And then they found it. The whale! Jaws wide open, the whale thrashed around, snapping its teeth at the monster. I crouched under my rock as the kraken moved closer, and for the first time, I saw its face. I clapped a hand over my mouth, swallowing back a scream.

Horned and full of snarling lumps, with huge white eyes on either side of its head, it opened its mouth to reveal teeth like shining daggers. Briefly opened wide, the teeth came crashing together, snapping shut, again and again, pulling and tearing at the whale. On and on it went, the whale flung from one side to the other as tentacles and horns and teeth grabbed and tore at its skin.

Eventually, the thrashing slowed. The whirlpool stopped. The sea began to change colour, blood seeping into the cracks around me. *Go away, go away*, I said silently, over and over, until, miraculously, the water became calm again, almost as though it had heard me.

In the darkness, I cried.

Mum.

I kept seeing her, reaching out to me from the ship, wild and screaming as she was taken further and further away. The image bit into me like wire. I curled into a ball and tried to push it away.

I had to find Mandy and her parents. They were my only hope now. I tore at the net till I'd made a hole big enough to squeeze through. Edging out of my hiding place, I forced myself not to think about what I'd just witnessed, although my twitching body made it hard for me to forget. I scanned the water. Nothing. It had gone.

Swimming away from the rocks, I searched desperately for something familiar. I soon came to a deep sandy stretch, rocks on either side. Around them, weeds floated and swayed, surrounding me like a thick curtain. I swam along the sandy channel until it came to a rocky reef, full of holes and ridges and grey peaks like castles and hills.

I fought the rising panic in my chest. This wasn't familiar at all. I was completely lost. A large, sullen grey fish drifted silently ahead of me, hovering like a hawk. Bright blue eyes bore down on me as I passed it.

'Who's that?'

A voice! A male voice.

'Come no further!' The voice called out again. I stopped swimming.

'Who are you?' My words bubbled away from me.

Silence. Then, 'You'll do as I say. I am armed. Do you understand?'

Armed?

'I – yes, I understand.' Understand? Of course I didn't! I didn't understand any of this.

Out of the shadows, a thin, lanky figure swam towards me. A young merman, maybe in his twenties. He pulled some fishing line out from a packet on his back. 'Hold your arms out.'

'Who are you? Why should I – '

'Do as I say!' he bellowed, reaching for something that looked like a knife by his side. I thrust my arms out in front of me and watched while he tied my wrists together. 'This way.'

With that, he turned and swam, pulling me along behind him. All thoughts of my mum and the kraken and Mandy were dragged away by this – my second capture in one day. I let myself be pulled along. What choice did I have? No strength left to fight, this time.

The reef stretched and curved, a lunar landscape dotted with ornamental gardens. Deep brown plants lined rocky chasms. Round boulder-like chunks of coral clung to every surface; thick green spongy tubes waved and pointed threateningly as we passed over them. I glanced at the merman as we swam. He had a thin grey tail with silver rings pierced all along one side. Wild blond hair waved over his shoulders, a chain made of bones hung around his neck.

We came to a cave with green and blue weeds hanging down from the top of its mouth in a curtain. Crystals were embedded in the rock all around the entrance.

'In here.' He pushed me forward.

'Where are we?'

'You'll see.'

Inside, the cave ballooned out into an enormous dome. Crystals, jewels and gold lined the route. Mosaics filled with gems of every colour swirled along the seabed; a round body, swirling arms ...

'Where are we?' I gasped. 'Who are you?'

'You'll find out soon enough,' he replied. We'd reached a building. It looked like a castle, or a ruin of a castle. Half-collapsed turrets were filled with diamonds; crumbling walls held pale jewels in clusters around their base. A giant archway for a door, a marble pillar on either side. As we came closer, I could see something embossed onto each pillar. A golden seahorse.

I knew this archway! I'd seen it before, or another one very much like it. 'This is one of Neptune's palaces, isn't it?' I asked, shuddering as I realised we were swimming over a mosaic shaped like a mass of tentacles.

The merman didn't reply.

Through the arch, a chandelier hung from a high ceiling, jangling with the water's rocking. That confirmed my fear. Neptune had found me.

We ducked low to swim through a smaller arch, adorned, like the others, with elaborate jewels. A wooden door lay ahead. The merman paused to neaten his hair. Then he turned a shiny brass handle and nudged me inside.

We were in a small room. A stone desk embedded with shells took up half the space. Conches and oyster shells lay scattered on its surface. Next to it, an old merman turned as we came into the room. He had a straggly beard and dark eyes that stared at me, holding me still.

'What's this you've found, Kyle?' the merman asked in a deep grumble. As he spoke, he stroked something lying very, very still by his side. It looked like a giant snake. Greeny yellow with purple teddy bear eyes, its gills slowly opening and closing as its mouth did the same, it swayed its head gently round to face me. A moray eel!

I opened and closed my mouth too, rigid with fear. Nothing came out.

'She was trespassing, sir,' Kyle answered briskly.

'Untie her. She won't try leaving here in a hurry, if she has any sense.' The old merman smiled at his pet. It leered back, stretching up almost as tall as him.

Kyle clenched his sharp jaw into a scowl as he pulled at the fishing line. I rubbed my wrists. 'Tell us how you got here,' he demanded.

'I don't know!' I said, tearing my eyes away from the eel. 'I don't even know where I am. I had an accident, got lost and you found me.' Then, trying to control the quiver in my voice, I added, 'Can I go home?'

'Home?' The old merman leaned towards me. The eel rolled its neck down into a spiral and closed its eyes. 'And where would that be?'

I looked away from him. 'Allpoints Island.'

The two of them exchanged a look. What was it? Shock?

'Allpoints Island?' Kyle blurted out. 'So you know about – '

'Kyle!' the old merman snapped. 'I'll handle this.'

'Of course. Sorry.' Kyle drew back, bowing slightly. Pausing briefly to pat the moray, the old merman swam towards me. 'Now then,' he said, in a voice as slimy as the eel. 'I don't believe we've been introduced. 'I'm Nathiel. And you are . . . ?'

'Why should I tell you who I am?' I said, my heart bashing against my chest. 'Why won't you let me go? What are you going to do with me?'

Nathiel laughed and turned away. 'Questions, questions. Where shall we start, Kyle?'

Kyle shuffled his tail, pulling on his necklace. 'Um . . .'

Nathiel waved him away. 'Very well, little girl. I'll tell you who we are. Seeing as you've been kind enough to drop in. We are your biggest fear . . . or your greatest protectors. Depending on how you view your situation at this moment.'

'You're not my biggest fear,' I said, my heart thumping. 'My biggest fear is much worse than you!'

'Oh yes?' Nathiel swam back towards me, no trace of kindness or favour on his face. He twitched his head and the eel rose up, uncoiling itself to slither along behind him. I flinched as it stretched almost up to my face.

'Do you know how powerful we are?' Nathiel asked in a quiet, biting voice. I shook my head quickly, without taking my eyes off the eel. 'We are Neptune's chosen ones, his elite force, the only ones he trusts with his most prized possession.' Nathiel edged a centimetre closer to me, his cold eyes shining into mine. 'We, little visitor, are the kraken keepers.'

A million questions jammed into my mind. 'The kraken keepers? But if you're, but it's – '

Nathiel laughed, a throaty sound that echoed around the room. The eel slowly stretched up. It was about three times taller than me. *Please don't open your mouth, please don't open your mouth,* I prayed silently as its jaw twitched.

With another click of Nathiel's fingers, the eel slithered to the back of the room, folding itself once more into a perfect coil.

'Now,' Nathiel said, 'that's my side of the introductions. I think it's time we heard a little more about you. You see, we know quite a bit about Allpoints Island, don't we, Kyle?'

Kyle swam forwards. Copying Nathiel's sneer, he replied, 'Neptune tells us everything.'

'That's right. So, for example, he tells us about merfolk who break his laws.' Nathiel swam further forwards. 'Merfolk who go meddling in places they shouldn't,' he added, edging closer still, his nostrils flaring. 'Merfolk who WAKE his beloved KRAKEN!' he shouted.

'But, I – how did you know?' I cried. My body was shaking. Water frothed around my tail. I tried to make it lie still.

Kyle stared at Nathiel. 'Yes. How did you?'

'I *didn't* know!' Nathiel replied. 'Swam right into

it, didn't she? Come on, Kyle. What do you get if you add the kraken on the loose, an island full of merfolk who know nothing about it and a scared merchild clearly running away from trouble? It's a simple case of mathematics.'

'So we've found her?' Kyle said.

'We've done good work.' Nathiel patted Kyle's arm. 'Neptune will be very pleased with us. Very pleased indeed.'

'Neptune? You're going to tell him?' My voice quivered.

'Of course! That is the whole point. Don't you realise the danger we are all in, you foolish girl?'

'But Neptune! He'll be furious with me.'

'You think we give a fin about that?' Kyle snapped. 'We need you. All of us. There's more than just yourself to consider.'

'What do you mean? What use am I to you?'

Nathiel shook his head. 'Kyle, I've had enough of this whingeing. I think it's time we got the boss in.'

'The boss? Neptune? He's coming here?' I squeaked.

'Not Neptune, no. One of his most trusted aides.' Nathiel picked up a conch. Turning away from me, he spoke softly into it. I couldn't hear what he said. I quickly scanned the room, looking for an escape. My eyes met the eel's. *Try it*, they seemed to say. I shivered back against the wall.

'He'll be along very shortly.' Nathiel put the conch down and tidied some shells on his desk.

A moment later, the door opened. I squeezed my eyes shut in terror. Someone was swimming towards me. I bit my lip as hard as I could, forcing tears away.

'Well, what have we here, then?' a voice said. A creepy voice.

A very familiar voice.

My eyes snapped open, to see a crooked smile, an odd pair of eyes: one green, one blue.

It couldn't be!

'Hello Emily,' said Mr Beeston.

He turned to the others. 'Good work, both of you,' he said, snapping something around my wrists. Handcuffs made from lobster's legs! They bit and scratched at me.

Then he pushed me towards the door. 'I'll take over now,' he said before turning back to give me another of his lopsided smiles. 'It's time we were reacquainted.'

How could they let this happen? Twice! I can't *believe* my parents! I can't believe I agreed to this stupid holiday in the first place.

We're hanging onto our useless, broken boat, lying across it, gripping onto ropes. Only problem is, it's upside down! How long before it sinks and we *totally* end our holiday in style? I grab the rope tighter as the swell carries us up and down. My stomach seesaws with it.

Are we through that, that whatever it was, that great big sheet of glass in the middle of the ocean?

And the other thing.

I refuse to think about it. It didn't happen. Mum and Dad haven't mentioned it. I must have imagined it. Delirious, that's what I am. It was probably just the waves. Or a vision, because I'd seen it before. A memory. Yes. That's it. Definitely. A mirage.

There's nothing to worry about. I'm just cracking up.

'Maureen, Mandy – look!' Dad lets go of the rope with one hand and points out to sea.

It's a ship. Coming towards us!

'Wave! Both of you! Splash your feet!' Dad yells. For

the first time in our lives, Mum and I do what he says without arguing.

The ship's coming closer and closer. Have they seen us? They *must* have! There's nothing except us moving for miles all around us. We're kicking and yelling, every atom of hope screaming out of us.

'I can't splash any more, Dad. My legs are killing me.' I stop kicking for a moment while I catch my breath. The ship's stopped moving. They haven't seen us, after all. That's it. There's nothing we can do now. The realisation slams into my mind like a block of ice: we're going to die.

But then I notice something attached to the ship.

'Look!'

They're lowering a lifeboat into the water! It's coming to get us.

We've been saved!

Chapter Seven

*M*r Beeston unhooked the lobster claws from my wrists and pulled out a couple of jelly-like cushions. He motioned me to sit down on one of them while settling himself on the other. I'd hardly ever seen him as a merman. He was half human and half merperson like me, the only other one I'd met. He looked just as creepy either way, with his crooked teeth and his crooked smile and the odd-coloured eyes that stared at you from the corners.

We were in a bubble-shaped room. It felt like the inside of a huge round shell. No windows, just one small hole divided by thick metal bars.

Tiny chinks of light threw pencil-thin beams across the darkness. A black damselfish with fluorescent purple spots and a bright yellow tail wove between the rays.

I tried to stay calm. My mind wouldn't stop racing, though. What were they going to do with me? Would anyone find me? Dad? Shona? Were they looking for me? And what about Mum and Millie? My heart ached at the thought of them on that ship. They'd be miles away by now.

'What are you doing here?' I asked in a daze. Among the millions of questions racing round in my head, it was the only one I could seem to form into words.

'Surprised to see me?' he asked, his voice slipping across the room like slime.

'Of course I'm surprised to see you! Who's looking after the lighthouse in Brightport?'

'The lighthouse?' Mr Beeston laughed. 'Emily, why would I be looking after a lighthouse?'

'It's what you do!'

'The lighthouse was a cover. You know that.'

'Oh, yes. Of course,' I said numbly. I'd found out before we left Brightport that Mr Beeston was one of Neptune's agents and that he'd been spying on us to make sure we never found out about Dad. Well, it didn't work, did it? I found my dad. I'd beaten Mr Beeston once. Maybe I could do it again. 'But that still doesn't explain – '

'I was promoted,' Mr Beeston said, a crooked grin

twitching at the side of his mouth. 'For my bravery and good work.'

'*Good work*?' I spluttered. 'Is that what you call turning me and Mum over to Neptune? You were meant to be our friend. We could have been thrown in prison, like my dad.' I squeezed my eyes shut and pressed my fingernails tightly into my palms. I wasn't going to cry. He wasn't having that satisfaction.

Mr Beeston flicked his tail nervously. 'I – well, Emily, I did my duty. And look, I was needed here. They're working on rebuilding this palace, and there's a lot to do, monitoring activity in the area and keeping a gill open for any kraken-related incidents.' He narrowed his eyes at me accusingly.

'So what are you going to do with me?'

'Do with you? It's not about what I want to do with you. It's about what you need to do for us.'

'What d'you mean?'

Mr Beeston shuffled forward in his cushion. I shuffled backwards in mine. He tightened his lips. 'I am still an agent of Neptune's, you know,' he said sharply. 'One of the highest ranking of all, now. And if I tell you that you are going to do something, you will do it. You don't question my authority.'

I folded my arms, anxiously flicking my tail while I waited for him to continue.

'We are all in grave danger. The kraken is on the loose. It has to be calmed and brought back to Neptune.'

'But what's that got to do with me?'

He held my eyes for a long time before replying.
'You, Emily, are the only one who can do it.'

Someone was banging on the outside of the shell. Mr Beeston opened the porthole-shaped door we'd come through. Kyle surged into the room on a sudden wave. It flung me against the wall.

'Sir,' he said breathlessly. 'I've had a sighting. It's coming closer. The sea – it's getting rough.'

'Thank you, Kyle. Good work,' Mr Beeston said.

'It's heading towards the palace!' Kyle panted. 'I think it's going to get us all. We might have to make our escape.'

'Make our escape? Are you off your fins, boy?' Mr Beeston barked. 'Have you been given the wrong job? You have one purpose and one purpose only. Do you hear me?'

'Yes sir.' Kyle reddened. 'I'm sorry.'

'Now, don't let it out of your sight. I'm dealing with it. Have some faith.'

Kyle retreated, leaving a swirling cloud of silt behind him.

'Are you going to explain any of this to me?' I asked as Mr Beeston swam back into the room. A tiny silver fish swam towards him, slithering across his stomach. He batted it away.

'The kraken is Neptune's pet,' Mr Beeston began.

'I know that.'

'And it sleeps for a hundred years. Without its full sleep, it wakes in a murderous rage.'

'I know that too.'

'Stop interrupting me, child! I shall tell you the story my way or not at all.'

I slammed my mouth shut.

'All but Neptune are forbidden to approach the kraken during its sleep. Neptune is the only one who should wake it. And only at the allotted time. You see, when it wakes, the only person it will listen to it is the one who wakes it, the one it sees first on opening its eyes. This should only ever be Neptune. But this time, it was you.'

'You mean ...?'

'Yes, Emily. The kraken will obey you and only you.'

I realised I wasn't saying anything. My mouth moved. Opened. Closed. Nothing. The kraken would obey me and only me? I slumped back against the wall, my mind empty, my limbs numb. A thin ray of sunlight threw a diagonal line across the room like a dusty laser beam, lighting up barnacles that lined the walls. The beam shimmered and broke, rocked by the water's constant movement.

'What do you want me to do?' I asked eventually.

'We need to move quickly. Neptune's power over the kraken is fiercely protected. It's not expected that anyone else would ever wake it. *Most* merfolk obey his rules.' He paused to scowl briefly at me. 'First, you have to go to the edge of the Triangle, where its magic is strongest.'

'The edge of the Triangle?' I gasped. 'You mean the torrent that leads to the deepest depths of the ocean?'

'Nonsense!' Mr Beeston snapped. 'It doesn't do that. That's what we tell folk to keep them out of the way.'

'So where does it go, then?'

'It leads into the realm of the kraken.'

'The realm of the kraken?' My voice cracked. Somehow, that didn't sound much more inviting than the deepest depths of the ocean.

'The place where you can communicate with it. You must go to the edge of the Triangle and come face to face with it.'

'Face to face?' I burst out. 'With the kraken?' I couldn't face the monster again. Please no! An image squirmed into my mind: those horrific tentacles, searching, batting and thrashing, smashing into the tunnel. My eyes began to sting with tears. I didn't care any more if Mr Beeston saw me cry. I couldn't hold it back.

He spoke softly. 'It's the only way.'

'What happens then?' I asked, swallowing hard. 'When we're at the Triangle's edge?'

'It will come to you. It will listen to you.'

'And I can save the day?'

'What? Yes, yes, of course you can save the day.'

'And it'll do what I tell it?'

'As I told you, it will listen only to you. Its power lies in your hands.'

I suddenly realised what Mr Beeston was telling me. I could end all of this. I could bring the kraken into my power. It would listen to me. I could calm it down and everything would be all right. I just had to face it one more time.

'OK,' I said. 'I'll do it.'

Mr Beeston smiled his crooked smile. 'I knew you would.'

He turned to leave. 'There's just one last thing,' he said, pausing at the door. 'You *were* on your own when you woke the kraken, weren't you?'

'I – why do you want to know that?' I blustered.

Mr Beeston darted back towards me. Coming so close that I could see the jagged points of his crooked yellow teeth, he leaned into my face. 'If someone else was with you when the kraken woke, we need them too.'

'Why?' I asked in a tiny voice.

'Emily, if there was someone else there, it means the kraken will not obey you on your own. Whoever it saw on waking, that is who it will obey – whether that is one person or twenty. We need them all or the plan will fail.'

'I . . .'

I couldn't do it. I couldn't! Not after everything. I wasn't going to drag Shona into this. They'd have to think of something else. 'There was no one,' I said eventually, my cheeks on fire.

Mr Beeston grabbed my arm, jerking my body like an electric shock. 'You're lying! You *have* to tell me. There was someone with you, I know it. Who was it?'

'I can't tell you!' I cried. Tears slipped down my cheeks. 'I can't do it! You can't make me.'

'Oh, I think you'll find we can,' he hissed.

I gulped. 'What if I refuse?'

Mr Beeston twitched slightly. 'Then the kraken won't stop until it has destroyed everything in its sight. These waves we're seeing – you know they're just the start of it.'

I thought back to what I'd seen: the kraken smashing up Mandy's boat, what it did to the reef, the rocks . . . the whale. But could I really make Shona face it again? Could I betray her like that? It would finish off our friendship forever.

'I – I'll think about it,' I stammered.

He swam over to the door. 'Don't think for too long, Emily,' he said quietly. 'Time is an option we don't have.'

Now, this is more like it! This is what our holiday was meant to be like all along. Luxury cruise liner, sunbeds, swimming pool, free drinks. We're even getting special attention from the crew because of our trauma.

Yeah, it's all great.

Except. Well, except Mum and Dad haven't spoken a word to each other since we were saved. The atmosphere's so cold when they're around, you'd think we were on a cruise to Antarctica. And neither of them even cares about me. They've hardly noticed me since we got here.

So it's not only that my home's about to be pulled down; my family's falling to pieces too. That's just great. We're back where we started, only worse.

And then there's Emily. Apart from wondering what she's doing here anyway, and not to mention the fact that she happens to be a *mermaid*, I just can't believe I let her get one over me, yet again.

We set sail again soon. They've been trying to get away from here, but there's something wrong with the ship. It keeps going off course for some reason. They're trying to sort it out, and once they have done and we're away from here, I'll *never* get a chance to repay her. She'll always have won.

For once, Dad had actually come up with a brilliant plan, and we let it slip away. If only I could find her. Kill two birds with one stone. Get fish girl back AND save our home. Now *that* would be satisfying!

Maybe I could. Who says it's too late?

I'm wandering round the back of the ship trying to think of something when I hear voices. Three people are standing near the lifeboats. One of them's waving her arms in the air, shouting at someone in a Carefree Cruises uniform.

'But why on earth can't you just let it down?' she's yelling. 'I know you used one of them to let a family come aboard. We have to get off the ship! I have to find my daughter!'

'Madam, they were in trouble. We couldn't leave them to drown,' the Carefree Cruises person replies. 'And you won't tell me anything about your daughter's whereabouts. You won't even give me your name. You can hardly expect me to break ship's regulations just because you and your friend here fancy a trip in a lifeboat.'

The other one looks up. That's when I see who it is. A big woman in a black cape. It's Mystic Millie, the crazy lady who used to read palms on the pier in Brightport! What the –

'A child is in trouble,' she says. 'That's all you need to know. We've seen things. *I* have seen things. And if you don't mind my saying so, I am rather known for the accuracy of my visions. Isn't that right, Mary Penelope?'

The other woman turns her head as she nods. I duck down behind a plastic box full of diving equipment before she spots me. But I've seen her face. It's Mrs Windsnap! What are they doing here?

They're moving away. I can't hear the rest of the conversation. But then a thought occurs to me. They want to get off the ship to find Emily. That means she must be near here somewhere.

I could get her! She's probably really near us. I could find her and then get one of those lifeboats to rescue me again. Someone's got to do something – and it doesn't look as though Mum and Dad are going to bother. Too busy ignoring each other. I'm absolutely *sick* of them.

It's not as if they'll even miss me. And if I get lost out at sea, well, they'll be sorry then, won't they!

I yank open the plastic box and rifle through the contents. There's all sorts here: lifejackets, rubber rings, inflatable beds, snorkels, masks, flippers.

Before I can talk myself out of it, I'm grabbing everything I'll need and clambering down a ladder that reaches almost down to the water. I'll do it. I'll get her back, save our home. I'll be a heroine. Mandy Rushton, the girl who single-handedly put Brightport on the map. Yes!

I drop into the water. For a second, the cold jams my brain. What am I doing? The ship's speeding away. Too late to change my mind. Oh God, what am I *doing*?

Then Emily's face comes into my mind and I remember. I pull the mask on and start swimming.

I can see all the way to the bottom of the sea. It's incredible: so clear, so blue. Tiny speckled fish, spongy purple and green plants, trees almost. It's a whole other world down here.

There's something else kind of nagging at me. A tiny voice is telling me not to do this. There's a threat down here.

But I'm not thinking about that. I refuse. It didn't happen. Mum and Dad would definitely have said something by now if they'd seen it. It's not exactly the kind of thing you miss. It was just a wave. A mirage. I was delirious. But I'm not now! I've never felt so clear-headed in my life!

I'm swimming away from the ship. She must be around here somewhere. She can't have got far – she was in a net. I swim on.

And on.

And on.

The rocky coral is just below me, all furry as though it's covered in dust and fluff. Pink, gooey, jelly-like clumps clutch at the rocks. A dull grey fish glides towards me. Then suddenly it flaps bright purple fins. It looks like an aeroplane with fancy painted wings.

Where am I?

I'm exhausted. There's no sign of her anywhere. I tread water for a bit while I adjust my mask and look round. That's when I realise how far away from the ship I've come. It's *miles* away. What am I doing? I've gone mad! I need to get back to the ship.

There's a plank of wood floating nearby. I've just got enough energy to reach it. It looks like a piece of our boat! My teeth chatter as I cling to it and try to work out what the heck I'm going to do next.

The water's really dark here, and murky. I dip under to look round but I can hardly see anything. The jelly stuff seems to be reaching higher, trying to grab me. And there are too many sea urchins.

And then I see something stringy, floating up towards the surface. I paddle over to examine it. It's a piece of net; I'm sure it's hers.

She got away then.

There's something else. Something very big. Black on top, white underneath, a giant fin on its back. It's coming towards me!

I want to scream. I know I want to scream – but I can't. I can't get anything out of my throat. I couldn't even if I wasn't underwater, in the middle of the sea, miles from anywhere. It's the monster! I knew it! I should have trusted my instincts. I'm an idiot. And now I'm a dead idiot.

Maybe I can get away before it eats me.

But it's not moving.

Yes it is. But not towards me. It's floating, gliding slowly upwards. And it's not the monster.

It's a killer whale. And it's dead.

As it floats past me, I watch with a morbid fascination. There's a chunk missing from its side. My body starts to shake.

Fear finally kicks in, and so do my legs. I am *so* out of

here! OK, fish girl, I surrender. You win. I don't care; I just want away from this place.

My legs don't seem to be working any more. Please just get me back to the ship! Please get me away from here. I'll do anything. I'll be nice to Mum and Dad; I'll even forgive Emily for tricking me. Just get me back to the ship alive! *Please!*

Something grabs my legs. That's it. I'm dead.

I don't even struggle. I can't. My body feels as useless as the half-eaten whale. I close my eyes and wait for –

'Who are you?'

What? I open my eyes. A man's face has appeared in front of me in the water. Young, almost a boy. He's gripping my arms. Where did he come from?

I open my mouth and swallow about a gallon of water. He waits while I splutter half to death and put my snorkel back on.

'Come with me,' he says.

Still holding my elbow with one hand, he pulls me along in the water. I catch a glance under the water as we swim – and that's when I see. He's not a man. He's a merman! He's got a long tail with silver rings all the way down.

We're heading towards something that looks like an island. As we get closer, I realise it's just a collection of rocks and caves. We swim among the rocks.

'Nathiel,' the merman calls. Still holding onto me, he yanks me downwards. I quickly adjust my snorkel so I can still breathe.

Below us, a rabbit warren of rocks and tunnels and

caves spreads out as far as I can see. It's like a city, packed with too many buildings crammed together as closely as possible.

An old guy with a straggly beard appears from inside a large crevice. Another merman! We come back up to the surface together.

'Another one?' he says.

'Another what?' I burst out. 'Have you got Emily?'

The young merman looks at the older one. 'Emily?' he says. 'Sharks alive, Nathiel – d'you think this is the one?'

The older merman turns to me. 'You're Emily's friend?' he asks.

'I – ' What has Emily got to do with this?

'You were looking for her!' he demands, shaking me.

'Yes!' I burst out. 'Yes, I'm looking for Emily. Is she here?'

'Kyle, tell the boss straight away,' the old merman orders. 'Take her to the Lantern Cave first. It's the only safe place above water.'

Kyle turns to swim away with me.

'No!'

They both swivel their heads to stare at me.

'Please,' I say. A tear streaks down my cheek. I don't care. Anyone would cry in these circumstances. Anyway, I'm not crying. It's the sun. It's shining right into my eyes. 'Please let me go home.'

'Where's home?' Kyle asks.

Good question. Home. You know, the place that's about to get pulled down, where I live with two people who can't stand the sight of each other.

'I need to get back to my parents. Please,' I blub like a baby. Have I really been reduced to this? Begging to be with my parents!

Nathiel says, 'And where are they?'

'I don't know.'

He turns to Kyle. 'Just get her to the Lantern Cave for now. We can always – '

'They're on a ship,' I say.

Nathiel snaps back to face me. 'What?'

'They're on a ship, over there somewhere.' I point back in the direction I think I came from. I sob. I can't help it. 'Please let me get back to it.'

The pair of them look at each other.

'A ship.' Kyle's eyes are shining. 'This is it! We need to move fast.'

What's he on about? 'Are you going to let me go?' I ask.

Nathiel turns to me, grips my shoulders. 'You want to go back to your ship?' he asks.

I nod.

'And you can show us where it is?'

'I – I think so.'

Nathiel lets me go. 'Handed to us on a plaice,' he says, smiling at Kyle. 'Good work.'

Kyle's cheeks flush. He doesn't speak again, just takes me towards a cave. I squeeze through the tiny entrance. It opens out when we get inside. It's dark, and creepy. I can just about make out strange shapes hanging down from the roof. Tiny chinks of light coming through holes way above me, huge boulders with brown gooey stuff that looks like toffee icing dribbled over them.

He closes a metal barred door and locks it from the outside. I grab the bars. 'Wait!'

'We'll look after you,' he says, his face cold and expressionless. 'Don't worry.'

Don't worry, I think to myself as he swims away from me. I climb out of the water onto a rocky ledge, my body shaking and cold. Sure. Absolutely. Why would I worry? I mean, I've only been locked in a dark cave on my own, with nothing but weird clumps of rocks hanging from the ceiling like enormous crooked fingers pointing at me.

I turn away from the pointing fingers. I've got to get out of here. I just need a plan. I'll think of something.

I shiver as the darkness closes around me.

Chapter Eight

I swam round my cell for the hundredth time.

'Let me out!' I yelled, scratching my hands down the rocky walls. My voice echoed around me. Finally, I slumped in the corner.

The next thing I knew, the door was rattling. I leapt up as Mr Beeston came in carrying a net basket filled with shellfish and seaweed. He placed it on a rocky ledge beside me. Water crashed around me as I reached for it, throwing me against the sides.

'See that?' he snarled as I grabbed the ledge to stop myself being thrown back against the wall. 'That's virtually constant now. And it'll keep getting worse, until you've done what you need to do.'

I didn't reply.

'Eat your breakfast,' he said, nudging a finger at the basket. 'You need to be strong.'

'I haven't said I'll do it.'

'No,' he said, his face breaking into an uneven smile. 'But *I* have.'

'I don't have to do what you say.' The edges of my eyes stung.

'Really? Well you won't be interested in our new visitor, then. Kyle tells me he's found someone who might make you feel differently.'

'A visitor?'

'A friend.'

I quickly rubbed my eyes. 'You've got her here? But how did you know – '

'Eat up quickly,' he growled in a voice that made my skin itch. 'It's time for a reunion.'

We swam up towards the surface, Mr Beeston's hand gripping my wrist so tightly it burned. The water grew lighter and warmer as we made our way along tunnels and out into clear water. He pulled me down under a clump of rocks, scattering a group of stripy triggerfish. A metal gate filled a gap between the rocks.

'Up there,' he said.

My heart thudded. I was really going to see Shona! But what if she wouldn't speak to me after everything that had happened? She'd probably hate me even more now, for being dragged into it again. I had to explain. 'Can I see her on my own?' I asked.

'What for?'

'It's personal.'

'Ah, friendship, so sweet,' Mr Beeston snarled, his throat gurgling into a laugh. He gripped my arm, his broken nails scratching my skin. 'You can have five minutes,' he said. Then he fiddled with a lock, and the gate bounced open. I swam through it, along a narrow crack. 'And don't try anything clever,' he called through the bars.

'I won't.'

I swam all the way up to the surface. I was inside a cave, in a tiny pool. Grey pillars lined the edges, their reflections sombre in the greeny blue water. A tiny shaft of sun lit up the stalactites hanging from the ceiling like frozen strands of spaghetti. Where was she?

I swam between the pillars, where the pool opened out. Slimy brown rocks lay all around. Thick clusters like bunches of candles protruded upwards from the water, black as though they'd been singed.

'Shona?' I called.

And then I saw her. Sitting on one of the rocks, her back to me.

But it wasn't Shona.

Her hair was short, and black. She turned round. For a moment, she looked shocked. Then she forced her angular face into a twisted smile.

'Hi there, fish girl,' she said. There was a smarmy look on her face, but I was pretty sure her voice wobbled a little. 'Long time no see.'

'Mandy!'

'Having fun?'

'Having *fun*? You think being captured and locked in an underwater tunnel is *likely* to be my idea of fun?'

'Oh, sorry. I didn't realise.'

'Didn't realise what?'

'That they didn't like you as much as me. Should have guessed though. I mean, people never do, do they?'

'What are you on about?'

'Oh, aren't they looking after you nicely? Haven't they promised to take you home?' She glanced at my face. 'Oops. Obviously not. Sorry. I always seem to say really hurtful things, *totally* by accident! Don't worry. You can't help it if people don't like you, can you?'

'Yeah, right, Mandy. I don't think so,' I said, clenching my hands into tight fists.

Mandy shrugged. 'Thing is, some of us understand how to get what we want; some of us don't. It's just the luck of the draw. Not your fault, I suppose.'

'You're lying.'

'Whatever.' Mandy picked up a stone and threw it

into the water. I watched the ripples grow wider and more faint. Then she stepped back up the rock and twirled round the pillars, prancing around the place as though she owned it.

'Why would they like you?'

She stopped prancing and glared at me, eyes wide open and innocent. 'What's not to like?'

'Where do you want me to start?' I spluttered.

Mandy frowned. 'Anyway, they're stupid,' she said quickly. Then she turned to look at me. 'Hey, that's a point. *They're* stupid and so are you. Funny that, isn't it? You'd think you'd get on a bit better, having something in common like that. Anyway, I don't care. They're taking me back to the boat soon.'

'Your boat? You didn't sink?'

'Not that old washed-out lump of tin,' she laughed. 'No, our new boat. Oh, did I forget to mention that we got saved by a luxury cruise liner? Funnily enough, they want to treat us like royalty, too! Shame, isn't it?'

'A cruise liner?' My voice suddenly shook. 'What cruise liner?'

'The one that we should have been on in the first place. The holiday we were *destined* to have. But not to worry. It's all OK now. They're taking me back later today.'

'Taking you back? But why?'

Mandy bit her lip before turning away. 'Told you. They like me.'

'Mandy, you can't trust these – '

A sound of metal on metal clanked below me. Mr Beeston appeared. 'Five minutes is up.'

'Why are you taking her to the ship?' I demanded.

'We're going together,' he replied.

'*Why?*'

'It's at the edge of the Triangle,' he answered quickly.

'How do you know? How do you know where it is?' I could feel the panic rising in my throat, edging into my voice. 'There's something you're not telling me! Why won't you *tell* me?'

'You know all you need to know,' he said. 'Let's go.'

'It's not Shona!' I yelled, pointing at Mandy. '*She's* not my friend! *Look* at her!'

Mr Beeston glanced across at Mandy as she turned round, and suddenly faltered. 'But that's, but you're – '

'*You!*' Mandy spluttered, looking up at him for the first time. 'Does someone want to tell me what's going – '

Just then, a huge wave rushed into the cave, filling it almost to the ceiling. Mandy lost her footing, slipping into the water beside me. I grabbed her.

'Get your hands off me, fish girl,' she spat. 'I can look after myself!'

'No you can't. You don't know what you're involved in!' I shouted.

Mr Beeston had disappeared under the water. A moment later, he resurfaced, fighting his way back up against the tide. I turned to face him. 'I'm not doing anything for you till you tell me exactly what's going on.'

'Want to bet?' he replied. Mandy opened her mouth to speak but a wave washed her words away. She spluttered and swam for the edge of the pool. Mr Beeston lunged towards me, grabbing my arm. I tried to struggle but he tightened his grip, his fingers scorching into my flesh as he pulled me back towards the grille at the bottom of the cave.

Mandy was shouting something as Mr Beeston pushed me out, fighting against the raging water. I couldn't hear her words any more.

'What are you doing with me?' I cried as a wall of white water rushed towards us, flinging me against a wall. 'What's going on? Tell me!'

'Don't you understand?' he shouted. 'We're *all* in danger here. Look at this. We can't live like this. You're the only one who can fix it.' We'd reached my cell. He yanked on my arm, pushing me inside. 'And you *will* do!'

Without another word, he turned and left. I heard the bolt slam across the door.

I slumped back against the wall and closed my eyes. How had it come to this? All I'd wanted to do was explore the island and make some new friends. How had I managed to cause such devastation? I looked round my dark cell. Shadows came and went on the walls as the hours passed and daylight faded, along with my hopes.

'Emily?'

Who was that? It sounded like . . .

'Emily!'

Dad? I swam to the door. '*Dad*!' I screamed.

The door burst open. It was! It was him. He wrapped me in his arms.

'How did you find me?' I asked, pressing into his chest.

'I – '

'Wait!' I pulled away from the door as I heard a noise outside. 'There's someone out there,' I whispered. 'How did you get past them?'

Dad took hold of my hands. 'Emily,' he said in a tight voice. He wouldn't meet my eyes.

'What? What is it?'

'They know I'm here.'

'They know? But how – '

'Archie,' Dad said simply. He looked briefly at my face and turned away again. Letting go of my hands, he swam round the cell. 'They came to see him,' he continued. 'Told him what had happened.' He ran a hand through his hair, pulling at it as he struggled to speak. Eventually, he looked up at me. 'He told me you hadn't been on your own.'

Suddenly it clicked. I felt as though he'd punched me. 'So that's why you're here,' I said. 'You just want me to tell you who I was with.'

Dad looked down. 'We've no choice, Em.'

My throat ached. He hadn't tracked me down, after all. He only came because he had to. Well, I didn't blame him. Why would he want me back after what I'd done?

Dad swam back towards me. 'Emily, I *begged* Archie to let me come. He wanted to do it himself.'

I didn't say anything. I couldn't. Lifting my chin, Dad spoke almost roughly. 'Remember when you found me, at the prison?'

I nodded, gulping a tear away.

'That was the happiest day of my whole life,' he said. 'Did you know that? And you know what was the worst?'

I shook my head.

'Last week, when I thought I'd lost you again.'

I held his eyes for a moment before falling back against him. 'Oh, Dad. It's been so awful!' I cried. 'They want me to face it again.'

'I know, little 'un, I know.' He held me tight while I sobbed.

'It was Shona,' I said eventually. I squeezed him tighter. 'What will you do?'

'We have to tell them, Emily. You don't know what it's been like at the island. Typhoons, giant waves. One side's totally devastated. All the trees knocked flat. Ships have come off their moorings, and it's only going to get worse.' Dad swallowed hard. 'There's something else I've got to tell you.' He held me away from him and picked up both of my hands. 'It's your mum and Millie. They went out looking for you, and we can't find them. There's folk out searching and I'm sure it won't be – '

'Dad! I know where they are.'

He jerked backwards. 'What?'

'I've seen them.' I told him about everything: the ship, Mandy, Mr Beeston.

Dad listened with wild eyes. 'Emily, there's no time to waste,' he gasped when I'd finished. 'We've got to do this. I'll send a message to Archie.'

'Don't leave me!' I gripped his arm.

'I'm not going anywhere,' he said firmly. 'I'll be by your side the whole time.'

'Do I really have to do this?' I asked, my voice quivering.

Dad held me close as he spoke into my hair. 'I'm sorry, Emily. It's the only way.'

That creepy Mr Beeston's pulling me along through the water on a kind of raft. I *never* liked him, back at Brightport. He's even worse now. He keeps shouting things to me. 'Where's the ship?' he bellows.

'I – I think it's – '

'WHERE'S THE SHIP!' he repeats, about ten times louder.

'It must have moved,' I call back to him. 'It was somewhere over there.' I point vaguely ahead of us.

'You know nothing, child,' he says. 'I don't know why we even brought you. No matter, we'll find it soon. It's probably already there.'

'Already where?' Emily calls. She's here too, with another merman. I think it's her dad. He keeps giving her these gooey sickly smiles.

'The edge of the Triangle. Same place we're heading.'

'You have to *tell* me!' Emily's screaming. '*Why* do you need the ship?'

'We're just getting our bearings,' Mr Beeston says.

Emily turns to the other merman. 'He's not telling us everything,' she whimpers. 'I *know* he's not. Why would they be taking Mandy home? It doesn't make sense.'

'Shh, let's just get there. We want your mum back. This is our best chance,' he replies in a quiet voice, glancing nervously at Mr Beeston. What are they up to? 'It'll be OK,' he says, holding Emily's hand. 'I'm here to look after you.'

Puke.

We swim on. I keep having visions of seeing Mum and Dad again. *Please get me to the boat. I promise I'll change. I won't be horrible any more.*

The water breaks in sharp waves all around us. It's getting really rough as we plough through enormous peaks and crash down into huge troughs. I'm grabbing the side of my raft, totally soaked.

And then I see it.

In the distance. On the horizon. I think it might be portholes, glinting in the sunlight. Yes, it is! A whole row of them! It's the ship!

'That's it!' I shout. 'Over there!' I point to the right.

We speed towards the cruise ship. I'm going to see Mum and Dad again! I'm going to be safe!

As we get closer, I can see its shape more clearly. And then it goes out of sight. There's something in the water, in front of the ship. It's like an island; a sickly khaki green island with hills and bumps. And it's moving. Long arms reaching up, propelling it forwards, blotting out the sun. I grip hard onto the raft as my stomach turns over.

The monster's going to get the ship.

I realise I'm screaming.

'Mandy, we can stop this!' Emily yells to me. 'They've told me I can calm it.'

'Why should I believe you?' I shout back. 'You think you're so special, don't you. Think you can do everything better than anyone else!' Tears are streaming down my face. Mum, Dad. They're so near and I'll never see them again.

'Listen to me!'

'No! I *won't* listen to you. If I hadn't been trying to find you, none of this would have happened! It's all your fault! Every single thing that's gone wrong here is YOUR FAULT!'

Emily doesn't speak again. Her face looks like it's been slammed between two walls. I don't care.

Why should I care? No one cares about *me*.

I'm going to die out here, and absolutely no one cares.

Chapter Nine

I gulped as we swam, trying to swallow, trying to breathe. Trying not to think about what I had to do.

Could I really calm the kraken's rage? Did I have any choice?

We were getting nearer to the ship – and so was

the kraken. The thought of Mum on the ship was all I needed to spur me on. I *had* to do it.

'Look!' Dad pointed at two shapes in the water. Archie and Shona!

Archie swam up to Mr Beeston, pulling Shona along with him. 'We've got her,' he said simply.

Mr Beeston nodded curtly. 'Just in time.'

Shona wouldn't meet my eyes. I didn't blame her. After everything I'd put her through, now she had to come face to face with the kraken again, and it was thanks to me – again.

Archie looked across at me. 'I'm glad you're safe,' he said, trying to smile.

'Safe? What makes you think I'm safe?'

'Come on. We've no time to lose.' He started swimming again, Shona joining me and Mandy as we trailed along behind the others. Dad swam up ahead with Archie.

'I'm not surprised you're not speaking to me,' I said as we sliced through the water.

Shona looked at me through heavy eyes. 'What d'you mean?' she asked. 'I thought you wouldn't be talking to me! I was so horrible to you. I've been a coward and a terrible friend. I wouldn't be surprised if you never want to speak to me again.'

I grabbed her hand as we swam. 'Shona, you weren't a terrible friend! If anyone was a terrible friend, it was *me*. I dragged you to somewhere you didn't want to go.'

Shona squeezed my hand. 'I should never have let

you take the blame. I'm so sorry,' she said. Then more quietly, she added, 'And so are Althea and Marina.'

'Althea and Marina?'

'They didn't think we'd really do it. They were scared of getting into trouble – that's why they kept out of your way. They feel dreadful. They wanted me to tell you they're going to make it up to you at the welcome party, when we get back.'

The welcome party. Were they still really going to hold a welcome party for us? Would I really ever be truly welcome there?

'We are friends again, aren't we?' Shona asked.

'*Best* friends! If you still want to be.'

She grinned.

'Well, excuse me for not joining in the happy moment,' Mandy burst in, 'but does either of you realise we're all about to *die* out here? Shouldn't we be trying to get *out* of this mess?'

'Mandy's right,' I said, suddenly realising Mandy and Shona had never met. Somehow, this didn't feel like the best time for introductions. 'We need to think about what we're doing.'

Ahead of us, the kraken had dipped underwater, an occasional tentacle lashing out across the surface. The sea bubbled with expectation.

Shona turned to me. 'What *are* we doing?'

That was a very good question.

We were there. The edge of the Triangle; the realm of the kraken. It was no longer a glassy plane over the ocean. An endless chasm stretched across the sea, giant waterfalls tearing down into the blackness below.

The ocean raged as the kraken surfaced in front of the chasm. Huge tentacles surged out of the sea, thick and lumpy, spraying water all around as they crashed onto the surface again and again.

I froze.

I couldn't do it.

Someone was shouting at me. I think it was Archie. It could have been Mr Beeston, or even my dad. It didn't matter. I couldn't change this, I couldn't face the kraken. I closed my eyes.

'The ship.' Mandy was pulling at my arm. 'The ship,' she said over and over again. 'It's going to sink the ship! *Do* something!'

The monster was looming over the ship as it edged towards the chasm. Tentacles reached high into the air. One swipe and it would all be over. 'MUM!' I screamed into the wildness, my eyes blind and blurred from tears and sea water.

Archie grabbed my arm. 'Face it!' he screamed. 'Both of you!'

'*Then* what?' Shona cried.

'Just do it! Face it together and be silent. Wait till it turns this way. I'll tell you what to do then. Quick!'

Shona turned to me.

'Come on,' I said. 'It'll be OK.'

I grabbed her hand and we turned to face the kraken together, waiting in silence for the awful moment when it would turn that long, hard, horrible face towards us.

And then it did.

Nothing else moved. The sea and swell stopped. The crashing waves leading down into blackness, the chasm – everything was still, held on a freeze frame. The kraken stood like a terrifying statue, motionless like iron, a giant tentacle poised over the ship, its bulging, weeping eyes locked with ours.

'It's working,' Dad whispered into the stillness. 'It's working!'

In the distance, a chariot was gliding over the water, pulled by dolphins. Neptune was on his way.

Archie glanced across at the chariot. 'You have to do it now!' he urged. 'Bring the kraken here, calm it down. Now!'

'What do we do?'

'Think.'

'Think?'

'In your minds, try to communicate with it.'

'*Communicate* with it?'

'Try to hold it in your power, bring it out of its rage so it can return to Neptune. You have to move fast.'

'OK.' I pulled at my hair, twirling it round as I flicked my tail. I glanced at Shona. She nodded quickly. OK. I just have to calm the kraken's rage. Think thoughts.

OK.

Calm down, nice kraken. I forced the words into my mind, my face squirming up with disgust and horror. A tentacle twitched, lashing out into thin air.

'You have to really feel it,' Archie said. 'It's no use pretending. It'll know.'

Neptune was coming closer. I had to do something before he got here, prove I wasn't completely and utterly useless, that I hadn't ruined absolutely everything. Shona's eyes were closed, her face calm and focused. OK, I could do this.

Please, I thought. *Please don't destroy anything. There's no need. Take it calmly, listen to us, trust us, it's all OK. No one's going to hurt you.*

Random thoughts raced through my head, anything I could think of that might have some effect.

And it did – it started to. The kraken's tentacles were softening, flopping back down onto the water, one by one. The swell of the sea had started shifting slowly, rising and falling steadily, the huge choppy waves with their sharp crests smoothing into deep swells. The chasm closed over, lying shiny and smooth like an oil slick.

'Good!' Mr Beeston called. 'Keep doing it!'

Don't be angry. Everything will be all right. Just be calm, calm, calm.

Beside me, I could almost feel Shona's thoughts, the same as mine, weaving in between my own words. The kraken was calming down. Its tentacles lay still and quiet, spread out across the ocean's surface.

The chariot was coming closer. I could see Neptune, rising out of his seat, holding his trident in the air.

'We've done it,' he cried as the dolphins brought him to my side. 'Bring it here. Bring it to me now. Only when it is right in front of you can you bring it fully back into my power.'

I swallowed. Here? Right in front of us?

'Now!' Neptune repeated.

I cleared my throat as I glanced at Shona again. Her face was white, her eyes wide and terrified.

I closed my eyes. *Come to us,* I thought, half of me praying it wouldn't work, the other half knowing that if it didn't we were all lost.

Nothing happened.

'You have to *mean* it!' Archie said. 'I've *told* you that.'

I took a deep breath and closed my eyes. Then, forcing myself to concentrate totally on my thoughts, I let the words come into my mind. *Come to us, now. We can end this. No more rage, just calm . . . come to us now.*

Something was happening in the water. Movement. I could sense it. I kept my eyes closed. *It's all right,* I said in my mind. *No one's going to hurt you. Just come to us now and we can work it out. Calm. Stay calm.*

'You're doing well,' Neptune said. His voice sounded as though he was talking right into my ear. 'Now, open your eyes. You have to come face to face with it, both of you. You need to hold it with your minds until the rage has completely gone.'

'How will we know when the rage has gone?' I asked.

'It will come back to me.'

I counted slowly to three, and then opened my eyes. It was all I could do not to scream from the top of my voice. It was there! In front of me! A face as tall as a tower block; lumpy and dark and pocked with holes and warts, tapering towards huge white eyes streaked with blood red veins. Enormous craggy tusks pointed up, disappearing into the clouds it seemed. Tentacles lay still all around it, like a deflated parachute.

I could hear cheering coming from the ship! The danger had passed. We'd done it. We'd really done it! I grabbed Shona's arm. She was laughing.

'We're not finished!' Neptune barked. 'Beeston, get ready. Archie, ready?'

'Yes, Your Majesty,' Archie replied, swimming away from me.

'Ready for what?' I asked. No one answered. Mr Beeston and Archie were swimming towards the ship. I grabbed Dad. 'Ready for what?' I asked again. 'What's going on?'

Dad shook his head. 'I don't – '

'What do you think?' Neptune growled. 'It's time to put it back to work.'

A queasy feeling stirred inside me. Something wasn't right.

'You don't think this is all merely to save your lives,

do you?' Neptune asked. 'Don't you think there is more to my kingdom than that?'

'I – I don't know. I don't under – '

'The kraken is getting back to work, as I've told you. It's been nearly a hundred years, and now it will return to what it knows best: relieving humans of what they do not need. It will bring me riches in quantities I haven't known for many years.'

What did he mean? He couldn't possibly –

'And that,' he pointed to the ship. ' . . . that is where we start.'

'But you can't!' I yelled. The kraken stirred as I shouted, a tentacle hitting the water with a splash that covered us all. 'You tricked us! You made us do all this, just so you can destroy everything!'

Mr Beeston turned in the water. 'We're not going to destroy everything. That's what the kraken would have done without you. We want to regain the control that is rightfully ours.'

'And the riches,' Neptune added, stroking a gold sash around his chest.

'Exactly, Your Majesty,' Mr Beeston added with a smarmy smile.

'Why didn't you just let it sink the ship then?' Shona asked.

'It will sink it for me! When I am ready. Otherwise, it is wanton destruction.'

'Wanton destruction?' I spluttered. 'And this isn't?'

Neptune's face bulged red. 'Without me, the kraken will destroy everything in its sight, losing it forever into the chasm. I will *not* suffer that waste!' He waved his trident in the air. 'Now go to it! I want every jewel from that ship!'

'But you'll kill them all!' I screamed, tears lashing down my face. 'My mum's on that ship!'

'Did we ASK her to be there?' Neptune boomed. 'Did we ASK you to start this?'

'But you can't just *kill* her! And Millie – all of them!'

Mr Beeston looked at Neptune, then me. 'Your mother's on the ship? What the – '

'I want my mum!' Mandy was crying next to me. 'I want to go home.'

'You can't!' I screamed at Neptune. 'Make it not happen – it can't be happening.'

The kraken twitched in the water, lifting a tentacle, tipping its head to the side.

'DO NOT lose it!' Neptune bellowed at Mr Beeston. 'We're too close. It's getting confused. We mustn't lose it now. Beeston, we need to sort this.'

'Please don't do it!' I cried uselessly.

Mr Beeston wouldn't look at me as he set off towards the ship. 'I'm sorry, Emily,' he said.

Dad lunged after him, grabbing his arm. 'My WIFE is on that boat!' he screamed.

Mr Beeston's left eye twitched. 'That – it's not our concern,' he stammered.

'Not your concern? Don't you care that people are going to die when you sink their boat?'

'Tough tails!' Mr Beeston suddenly exploded.

'They shouldn't stray into Neptune's kingdom. He is the ruler; everything in the ocean is his. He is only regaining what he's owed. Humans have stolen from him for centuries, poaching his seas for their own needs. We're just redressing the balance.'

He was mad. They all were.

Something was happening in the water. The kraken's tentacles were twitching, batting the water, spraying us all.

'OBEY ME!' Neptune screamed. 'It's caught between your control and mine. We have to combine them or it will go insane.'

'We won't!' I yelled back. 'We WON'T obey you!'

I grabbed Shona and Mandy. 'Come on!'

Mandy pulled away from me. 'Look what you're doing!' she shouted. 'You're making it *worse*!'

She was right; the kraken was coming back to life, tentacles rising to smash against the water.

'It's going to kill *everyone*!' Mandy yelled. 'You have to stop it!'

'Then what? If we obey Neptune, it'll go back into his power again, and he'll make it sink the ship anyway!' I cried. 'What can we do?'

It was ahead of us. Mr Beeston was calling it to the ship. No!

The kraken lashed forwards, tearing a hole through the sea as it spun towards the ship. The Triangle's surface was opening up again!

And then. And then.

I saw it in slow motion.

A tentacle, rising into the air, water spiralling off around it in an arc of colour and light. It came crashing down onto the water, hitting out, thwacking at the surface, swiping at the ship. The ship! It was so close. I could see people lined up along the decks, running madly, but there was nowhere to run. The tentacles rained down. It had the ship! It knocked at it, mad and hungry for destruction. The ship was tilting, people tossed from the deck – hundreds of people in the water, screaming for their lives.

'MUM!'

I whirled towards the kraken, edging towards the chasm; I could feel it pulling me – something holding us together; I couldn't fight it.

For a split second, everything stopped. The calm came back. The kraken had disappeared under the water. In silence, I watched the chasm close up, covered over again with the glassy surface of the sea.

Just one brief moment of calm, before a screeching wail split the air around us. Lights flared. The glassy surface splintered and cracked. The torrent raged below. And the kraken rose. It burst through the water, screaming up from deep below the surface, its long face stretched wide by angry, gaping jaws, dagger-like teeth, tentacles scrambling madly like a mass of giant maggots, smashing the still surface of the sea. As we watched, the water fell away, pouring like a waterfall, leaving just the kraken, surrounded in its fury by utter, black emptiness.

'We've lost our power,' I said feebly, to no one. 'It's not listening.'

I was being dragged towards the kraken. I could feel its mind pulling me towards it. Nothing I could do.

I couldn't save anyone. This force pulling me was too strong. No energy, no power to do anything.

I let myself slip towards the chasm.

And it closed behind me.

Down, down, into complete darkness. Nothing to see. No water, no land. Nothing. Falling through nothingness. Spiralling down, whisked round in a vacuum of whirling blackness, twisting me, throwing me round and round.

It grabbed me.

Lashing at me, scorching my face, my hands, my body, the kraken's tentacles screamed across me, again and again. I writhed and struggled, but it was imposs-ible. I couldn't keep out of its clutches.

I touched something that felt like jelly. With shud-dering, horrified disgust, I realised it was the edge of a sucker the size of a dinner plate. I gripped my body, trying to curl into a tight ball of nothingness.

'Why are you doing this?' I shouted uselessly as sticky, slippery tentacles slithered across my body, creeping around my tail, round and round, pulling me into a locked coil. I couldn't move a single thing. Brown hairs brushed across my face, writhing like a nest of worms. Terror sucked my breath away.

What could I do to stop it? Beg? What could I say? Why wasn't it *listening*? I'd woken it up! It should be in my power!

My thoughts rambled uselessly as tears lashed down my cheeks.

The tentacles reached higher and tighter, wrapping me up, trapping my arms, climbing up my body, finally closing over my neck.

This was it. This was where it ended. No one to save me.

The darkness slowly grew darker.

The ship's safe! It's all stopped. The monster's gone. But the people are still in the water. Loads of them. Someone's got to save them.

'What have you done with her?' Emily's dad is screaming at the really tall merman in the throne. 'What have you done with her? Give me my *daughter*!'

The big merman waves this great big fork thing around. 'Do you DARE question me in this manner?' he yells at the top of his voice. What is his *problem*? Can't he see people are in *trouble* here?

'Give her back to me!' Emily's dad howls, his voice cracking. 'Give her *back*!'

'We can't,' the big merman answers. 'The kraken has her.'

There's uproar after this. The merman's yelling. Some of the people from the ship have broken away. They're swimming towards us, shouting, calling things. They're coming closer.

'MANDY!'

It's Mum! My mum's in the water! I try to paddle my raft towards her. I can't get away. Mr Beeston's tied it up to that stupid chariot thing.

'Mum!'

What if that massive hole opens up again? What if it sucks us *all* in?

Someone's calling Mum from one of the lifeboats. She hovers in between us.

'Get in the boat!' I yell.

'Stay there, Mandy!' she shouts to me, swimming back to help the others. 'I'll get them to come for you.'

I nod, swallowing hard as I cling to my raft.

I can't stop thinking about Emily, in there with that thing. I can't let it happen. Was she honestly that bad? What did she ever really do to me?

Maybe I was wrong. Maybe she never had it in for me. It was always me who had it in for her. It was me who tripped her up in swimming, and called her names and stole her best friend. What did she do wrong, exactly? So, a few people liked her more than they liked me. Could I really blame them? *I* like her more than I like me at times.

I edge towards the big merman in the chariot.

'Please,' I beg. 'You have to do something. She's going to die in there.'

He turns slowly round towards me, looking down on me as though I'm an ugly beetle that's just crawled out of the sea. 'What am I expected to do about that?' he says, his eyes flickering towards the chasm. He looks away from me. 'I didn't cause it. She brought it on herself.'

'But can't you end it? Make the monster stop?'

'I cannot and I WILL not. Now leave me al–'

'HOW DARE YOU!' Someone suddenly shouts from the other side of the chariot. 'Give me a leg up will you, Jake,' she says in a quieter voice to Emily's dad. Then she hauls herself up onto the chariot. Millie! It's Mystic Millie!

The merman glares at her. 'Don't you know who I am?' he asks, his voice rumbling like an approaching typhoon.

'Yes of course. You're Neptune,' she says. 'But that – '

'KING Neptune!' he booms.

Millie presses her lips together, sucking on her teeth. 'Look, you could be King Kong for all I care,' she says, squeezing out her long black skirt over the sea. 'That still doesn't give you the right to let a poor innocent child get eaten by your precious monster.' She stares into his eyes and pulls something out from under her cloak. It looks like a gold pendant. 'Now are you going to do something about it?' she asks in a low drawl.

He stares back, his eyes flickering to the pendant. No one says anything. As he glares at her, something changes in his eyes. It's as though a flame starts to flicker behind them.

'Well, I . . . ' he says.

Millie moves closer to him. 'You know, even the greatest among us are allowed to change our ways if we want to,' she says quietly.

Then there's splashing in the water behind me.

'Mandy!'

It's Dad!

He's panting hard. He grabs me, clutching onto the

raft. 'Thank God,' he says. 'Thank God.' He's crying. I've *never* seen my dad cry. 'We've got to do something,' he says, his words coming out in rasps. 'Too many people in the water – not enough boats – someone's got to help.'

'Where's my *wife*?' Emily's dad gasps. He reaches up to grab Millie's hand. 'Make him do it,' he croaks. 'Get my daughter back. Promise me!'

Millie folds a hand over his. 'We'll get her back, Jake,' she says. 'I promise.'

He dives under the water and heads towards the ship.

I pull away from Dad. 'PLEASE!' I scream at Neptune. 'There has to be something we can do.'

He lifts his fork thing in the air again. 'Leave me alone, all of you,' he says. 'I do not need this. I will make MY decisions. I will NOT be influenced by ANY of you. If I choose to change my mind, it's not because of anything that you have said to me. Do you hear me?'

'Yes, yes, anything!' I scream.

Millie rolls her eyes, slipping her pendant back inside her cloak. 'Whatever you say,' she says with a frown.

'Well, then,' says Neptune, 'there is one last thing that may calm its rage and release the child. It comes from an ancient rhyme. It has never been used.'

'Why not?' I ask.

'Once its magic is invoked, I lose my power over the kraken forever. It will never return to its old ways. It will be a passive, weak shell of its former self.' He frowns in disgust.

'But the old days are gone. Surely you can see that! We can't cause death just to bring you jewels,' I say, adding more quietly, 'not that you're likely to even find a whole lot of jewels on that ship anyway.'

'So your ways are *better*, are they?' he snaps. 'Only the guilty die in your world, do they? Only for "good" reasons?'

'No, but . . . ' My voice trails away.

He waves me away. 'But I will not stand by and see this happen. You may be right. Perhaps we will find a different way. Let's get that girl out of there.'

'What's the rhyme?' Millie demands.

Neptune lifts his eyes to the sky.

'When old hatred's rift is mended
Thus the kraken's power is ended.'

'That's it?' My dad yells. 'A *nursery* rhyme? That's ridiculous! You said you were going to sort it.'

They're all shouting again. But I move away. Can I do something? *When old hatred's rift is ended.* I've hated Emily Windsnap for years. Maybe I don't have to any more. I could change this, do something good. Can I?

She communicated with the kraken just with her mind, didn't she? Maybe I can do the same, somehow. I'm going to do it!

I close my eyes and think of Emily, then I force a thought into my mind:

I'm sorry.

I say it over and over again in my thoughts. And then I wait.

Nothing.

What was I expecting? More flashing lights? I should have known nothing would happen. Nothing ever does when I try to do something good.

She's dead. The kraken's killed her. And I never had the chance to say I'm sorry.

I can see her in my mind. A picture from years ago. We used to play on the pier together. We were almost best friends. Why did I let her slip away?

Years of sorrow well into a tight ball, pressing against my throat.

But then –

I forgive you.

What was that? Who said it? I look around. No one's near me. They're all too busy shouting at each other, arguing over where to find the old hatred that they have to mend. I swipe a hand across my cheek, wiping away tears and sea water as I listen hard.

I forgive you.

It's Emily. It's her voice. I can hear her, again and again.

And then the chasm opens. It's starting again. It's whirling, throwing water around everywhere, splashing us all. A giant wave heaves towards us, knocking me off the raft.

'MANDY!' Dad yells, lunging for me. He swims away from the current, grabbing the raft and dragging us both back onto it.

'Please, no!' he sobs. 'Don't let me lose you.' He holds me tight, clutching my face to his chest as we kneel together on the raft.

When did my dad last hold me like this?

Over his shoulder, I can see the ship – but it's on the other side of the chasm. How will we ever get back to it?

As I stare into the raging water, all thoughts are suddenly swept from my mind. The monster's coming out of the sea again. Its head bursts out through the surface, scratched and veined with black lines, pus oozing out of crater-like holes in its skin. Piercing sounds of agony fill the sky.

Tentacles lash everywhere – it's out of control, screaming, on and on, the screeching siren sound. Roaring with anger, the monster lashes out again and again. And then I notice something in one of its tentacles. Emily! It's got her, holding her tight, throwing her into the air, crashing back down to the surface. She looks so tiny, like a little doll.

Please don't kill her . . . She's my friend.

Instantly, one final piercing scream shoots out from the water, exploding like a bomb, sending colour and water everywhere.

And it gradually quietens, slows. Stops. The giant waterfall stops raging. It's just a giant hole, spreading and cracking in a line through the ocean.

The monster crashes down onto the water and lies still, tentacles like bumpy highways, bridging the long well, jerking slightly, its head half sunk in the water. The sea fills with colour, purple lights flowing out of the kraken, seeping into the water all around us.

No one speaks. We hover in the sea, in silence, focused on the sight in front of us: the monster lying still, no one moving an inch.

We've done it. We've really done it.

Chapter Ten

J was having the cruellest dream. It started off as a nightmare. The kraken had me. Trapped and half strangled, I was in its clutches under the water. Then I heard a voice: Mandy, apologising. I thought, yes, let's make friends, I'm going to die any second now anyway.

And then it changed. I was above the water, in the air, thrown high by the kraken. But it let go of me and I came crashing back down onto the water, sinking, then rising back up to the surface.

The worst part was what happened next.

It was the best part really, but so cruel.

I dreamed my mum and dad were there. They'd come to save me. Shona was with them. We were best friends again. Even Mandy Rushton was there, and they were all asking if I was OK. No one was angry with me. All those eyes, looking at me with concern, helping me, carrying me somewhere, forgiving me for all the awful things I'd done. I wanted to call out to them, touch them, but I couldn't move; I couldn't speak.

I can't remember what happened next.

'Emily?'

'She can't hear you.'

'She's opening her eyes!'

Mum? I blinked in the sunlight. 'Mum? Is that really you?' I asked shakily.

She leaned over me, rocking as she held me tight. 'Oh, Emily,' she whispered into my neck, her voice choked and raw.

As she pulled away, I rubbed my eyes to see Dad's face next to hers. He was leaning out of the water, reaching up to hold my hand.

Shona was in the water next to him, smiling at me. 'You're OK!' she said.

I looked round: gold and jewels beside me, dolphins at the front. I was in Neptune's chariot! And I wasn't on my own. Millie stood at the front, talking in a low, deep voice. I knew that tone. She was hypnotising someone! But who?

'Now, moving your tentacle very, very slowly, lift another person out of the water,' she said softly, 'And carry them across the chasm, placing them gently on the deck of the cruise ship. Good, good . . .'

The kraken was doing what she said.

I shuddered as I remembered being in its clutches, the horror of its tentacles around my neck . . .

'We did it, then?' I asked numbly.

Shona beamed at me. 'You're a heroine, Emily. How could I ever have been angry with you? I'm such a jellyfish at times. Do you realise what you've done?'

'I – no. I don't know.'

I knew one thing, though. Whatever I'd done, I hadn't done it on my own. I pulled myself up. 'Where's Mandy?'

Shona pointed out to sea. 'She's on her way back to the ship,' she said. 'I think they'll be setting off soon.'

I got up, shakily. I had to see her. My legs wobbled.

Mum grabbed my arm. 'Emily, you need to rest.'

'Later,' I said. 'I've just got to do something.' Before she could stop me, I dived into the sea. I waited for my tail to form. It wobbled and shook just like my legs had done, but I could move it. I could get there. I had to see Mandy.

'I'm coming with you then.' Shona swam over to my side.

We made our way towards the edge of the Triangle. I gasped as I saw what lay ahead: a gulf of utter black emptiness. My body shuddered violently as I looked down. Across the chasm, the kraken reached a tentacle from one side to the other and out towards the ship, carrying people carefully across.

'I can't!' Mandy was screaming. 'It's HORRIBLE!'

'Quick! Come on. It's the only way across.' Her dad held his hand out to her. Mandy climbed up onto her awful slimy bridge. My body shuddered. I couldn't go near it!

She tiptoed along the tentacle. It was so huge it almost looked like a road, bridging the emptiness below. By the time I got there, she was nearly across.

'Mandy!'

She turned. The tentacle was starting to slip. Two more steps and she'd be there.

'Emily,' she said.

I swallowed. 'Thank you.'

Two steps away. She paused, stared at me. And then she smiled. I'd never seen her smile before. Not like that anyway. The only smile I'd ever seen from her was a sarcastic sneer. This one suited her better. It looked nice. Made her look like someone I might want to be friends with.

'Yeah, well,' she said. 'I didn't really do anything.'

'No, you're wrong.' I smiled back at her. 'You did a lot.'

Then she lurched across the tentacle, making her way back to the ship.

They'd gone. All of them back on the ship.

As the kraken lay still, I noticed someone in the water beside it. Tall, proud and silent, Neptune bent forward to stroke a tentacle, holding it sadly. Then he turned and looked around him.

'Beeston!' he called. Mr Beeston swam towards us from the ship.

'Have you completed the memory wipes?'

'Every last person, Your Majesty.'

Neptune nodded. 'Good work.' Then he clicked his fingers. Instantly, his dolphins squirted water in the air and dived down to pull the chariot through the water. Neptune clambered aboard.

'It's over,' he said. 'The kraken is falling back into its sleep. Who knows when it will wake now, or if it will even wake at all.' He beckoned Mr Beeston. 'We need someone to take on the responsibility of watching over it.'

Mr Beeston's mouth twitched into a crooked smile. 'Do you mean . . . ?'

'Who else could I trust with such an important task?'

Neptune looked round at us all. 'The rest of you will return to your lives. The kraken keepers will join you at Allpoints Island and you'll live together. The Triangle shall be sealed when I have left. Now, back to your island, everybody, and try to keep out of trouble this time.'

The ship was almost out of sight, a silhouette slowly gliding along the horizon.

Dad put an arm round me. 'Come on then, little 'un.' He nodded towards Allpoints Island as he pulled me close. 'Ready to go home?'

Shona caught up with us, linking an arm in mine. Mum and Millie smiled at me from inside the lifeboat.

Home. I thought about our bay, about *Fortuna*, Barracuda Point, the Grand Caves, mermaid school, the million things I hadn't yet discovered about All-points Island – and everyone waiting for us. Althea and Marina, and all my other new friends.

'Yes, I'm ready,' I said eventually. Then I turned to Shona and smiled. 'We've got a party to go to.'

The Brightport Times – 25 March

LOCAL HEROES SAVE BRIGHTPORT PIER

Brightport Town Council today voted unanimously to retain and modernise the town's historic pier. The decision came after local residents Jack and Maureen Rushton made a substantial donation from their recent windfall.

The Rushtons came into the money with their stunning photographs of a raging sea monster on the open ocean. The photographs have been sold to newspapers across the world.

The photographs were taken whilst on holiday with Mermaid Tours. Bizarrely, the couple have no recollection of their holiday.

'We were as surprised as anyone when we got the pictures developed,' Mrs Rushton said.

The Rushtons plan to expand their amusement arcade on the pier and are currently in negotiations with planners about a theme park which they will open later this year. The star ride will be a massive rollercoaster with a multitude of twists and turns along tentacle-like tracks.

The ride is to be called The Kraken.

Behind the scenes of the

Windsnap World

with Radio Merwave

Simon: Mandy, welcome to the show.

Mandy: **Cheers, thanks. Good to be here.**

Simon: Now then, before we do anything else, let's clear something up for our listeners. You and Emily Windsnap – you've got some history, right?

Mandy: **(Laughs.) Yeah, you could say that.**

Simon: So how about telling our listeners your side of the story?

Mandy: **All right, well, we used to be quite good friends ...**

Simon: Yes.

Mandy: **We hung out and played together quite a bit. We lived near each other and saw each other** most weekends. Sometimes we'd go to her place – her little boat. More often, we'd play at mine.

Simon: You live in an apartment on the pier, right?

Mandy: Right. My parents own an amusement arcade under the apartment, and Emily and I would sometimes hang around there, watching people play on the machines and keeping an eye out for the odd penny that they left behind.

Simon: Sounds good so far. So what went wrong?

Mandy: One day I noticed a coin stuck in the slot of the one-armed bandit. I tried to get it out but it wouldn't budge. Then I realised that the machine was showing a credit. I had a go, but it still showed a credit available. I think the coin had jammed it up, so the machine just kept acting as if more money had been put into it.

Simon: Then what happened?

Mandy: Emily came round that afternoon and I showed her the machine. We spent all afternoon playing on it! It was probably one of the best afternoons of my life, now I think about it.

Simon: But it didn't stay that way?

Mandy: Uh-uh. That night, Emily's mum came over to see my parents. I don't know exactly what was said, but once she'd gone, my mum and dad spent the rest of the night screaming at me.

Simon: Why?

Mandy: They said they hadn't spent their whole lives working just so that I could cheat them out of their profits. They said I was no better than a thief. And then they grounded me for a month. I kept trying to tell them that we'd only won about seventy-five pence, but they didn't care. They just carried on being mad at me.

Simon: And you blamed Emily?

Mandy: You bet I blamed Emily! Next day at school, I went straight up to her and asked her what she'd done. She said she'd never meant to get me into trouble. She'd been excited about having such a fun afternoon. Her mum had asked what she was so chirpy about. Plus she did have a pocketful of pennies, and her mum wanted to know where they'd come from – so Emily told her.

Simon: Oops.

Mandy: Yeah.

Simon: And then?

Mandy: And then we didn't speak for about a year.

Simon: Some people might say that you didn't exactly not speak to her . . .

Mandy: Yeah, I'm not proud of myself. I said some mean things. I wasn't very nice.

Simon: Some people might say you bullied her.

Mandy: I hate that word. But I don't blame people if that's the word that comes to mind. There's no excuse for the way I behaved. All I can say is that I was hurt. I thought that Emily had deliberately got me into trouble. And she had no idea how much trouble I'd got into – how angry my parents can be. It was the first time in years that they went for days without shouting at each other. They were both too busy shouting at me!

Simon: Sounds horrible.

Mandy: Yes, it was. But it's still no excuse for how I behaved. So, Emily, if you're listening, I just want to say it again – I'm really sorry. And I'm really glad we made up.

Simon: So that leads me on to my next question. How does it feel now that you and Emily have made friends again?

Mandy: The day Emily and I made friends again was the best day of my life! It just feels so cool to have put all that stuff behind us, and even cooler to think that by becoming friends again we managed to do something so great, and save lots of people's lives.

Simon: You're something of a heroine now!

Mandy: I wouldn't say that! But I like the way

people treat me now a lot more than I liked the way people treated me over the last year or so.

Simon: How is it different?

Mandy: Before, they only hung around with me because being my friend seemed less scary than being my enemy. Now, they're hanging around with me because I'm a nice person to be with. And that feels good. And being friends with Emily again reminds me of the old days. We have had a lot of laughs together over the years, you know. A lot of good times.

Simon: Like what? Tell us about some of them.

Mandy: Like going out on our bikes, and seeing who could cycle furthest along the prom with no hands.

Simon: Who won?

Mandy: I did, of course!

Simon: What else?

Mandy: Scrambling up the coast path on a Saturday afternoon to have a picnic. We called it a 'bic-nic' actually, as the only thing either of us had brought was biscuits!

Simon: Sounds ideal to me!

Mandy: Yeah, it was. We swapped secrets and made animal shapes out of the clouds, and dared each other to do stupid things like eat a biscuit while singing a nursery rhyme backwards! I hope we get to do all that stuff again one day.

Simon: It sounds like great fun! OK, so before you go, let's have some quick-fire questions. What's your favourite colour?

Mandy: The blue of the sky at Allpoints Island. I'm going to look for some paint in that exact colour when we get home, and paint my bedroom with it to remind me of the island.

Simon: Best memory?

Mandy: The day we heard we'd won a cruise holiday.

Simon: Worst memory?

Mandy: The day we saw our supposed cruise ship!

Simon: Hmm, yes.

Mandy: No, actually, my real worst memory was when I thought the kraken had killed Emily. I'll never forget how that felt – or at least, I hope I won't.

Simon: Favourite food?

Mandy: Fish and chips from Brightport Chippie. That's the first meal I'm having when we get home!

Simon: Favourite hobby?

Mandy: **I've never really had any hobbies, but I think I might take one up now. I want to start going fishing with my dad. These last few days have made me appreciate my parents more.**

Simon: And finally, describe yourself in three words.

Mandy: **(Pause.) Willing to change.**

Simon: Excellent! Well, listeners, I hope you've enjoyed today's behind-the-scenes interview. Mandy, thank you very much for joining us, and best of luck with your journey back to Brightport.

Mandy: **Thank you. Bye.**

Don't miss Emily Windsnap's
next exciting adventure

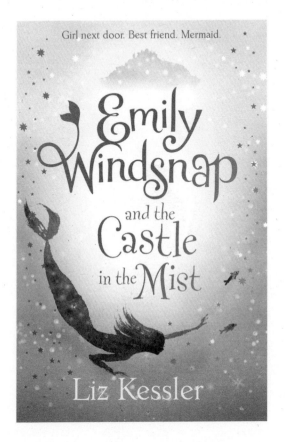

Girl next door. Best friend. Mermaid.

Emily Windsnap
and the Castle in the Mist

Liz Kessler

Read on for a special preview
of the first chapter

Prologue

*I*t's midnight, and as light as day.

A full moon shines down on the ocean, making the waves dance as they skirt the edges of the tiny island, lapping on to jagged rocks and stony beaches.

A chariot glides through the sea, tracing a circle around the island. Solid gold and adorned with jewels on every side, the chariot is pulled by dolphins, each decorated with a row of diamonds and pearls along its back and head.

Inside the chariot sits the king of all the oceans: Neptune. Grander than ever, a chain of sparkling jewels around his neck, his gold crown glinting above his white hair, his trident by his side, his green eyes shine in the moonlight as he looks across at the island. He is waiting for his bride to appear from the castle that stands above the rocks, half hidden by mist, its dark windows gleaming in the bright night sky.

'Go around again!' he demands, his voice booming like thunder. His words send ripples bouncing away from the chariot. The dolphins draw another circle around the island.

And then she is there, smiling as she steps towards the water's edge, her eyes meeting his, their gaze so fierce it almost brings the space between them to life. A bridge between their two worlds.

A small flock of starlings approach the water as she does, circling the air above her head like a feathered crown. Twisting her head to smile up at them, she holds out a hand. Instantly, one of the birds breaks off from the circle and flies down towards her open palm. Hovering almost motion-less in the air, it drops something from its claw into her palm. A diamond ring. As the woman closes her hand around the ring, the starling rejoins the other birds and they fly away into the night, slinking across the sky like a giant writhing snake.

'I give you this diamond to represent my love, as great as the earth itself, as firm as the ground on which I stand.' The woman flicks back shiny black hair as she reaches out towards the chariot to place a ring on Neptune's finger.

A twist of the trident and a dolphin swims forwards. As it bows down to Neptune, it reveals a pearl ring, perfectly balanced on its brow. Neptune takes the ring. Holding it out in his palm, he speaks softly. 'And with this pearl, I offer you the sea, my world, as boundless and everlasting as my love for you.' He slides the ring on to her finger. 'This is a most enchanted moment. A full moon at midnight, on the spring equinox. This will not happen for another five hundred years. It is almost as rare as our love.'

She smiles up at him, her white dress wet at the bottom where she stands in the sea by his chariot.

Holding his trident in the air, Neptune continues. 'These rings may only ever be worn by two folk in love – one from the sea, one from land – or by a child of such a pair. As long as they are so worn, no one can remove them.'

'No one can even touch them,' the woman says, smiling.

Neptune laughs. 'No one may even touch them,' he says. Then he holds his other hand up, palm facing the woman. She does the same and their arms form an arch, the rings touching as they clasp hands. A hundred stars crackle in the sky above them, bursting into colour like fireworks. 'When the rings touch like this,' Neptune continues, 'they will undo any act born of hatred or anger. Only love shall reign.'

'Only love,' she repeats.

Then he spreads his arms out in front of him. 'At this moment, night and day are equal, and now, so too are earth and sea. For as long as we wear these rings, the symbols of our marriage, there will always be peace and harmony between the two worlds.'

With a final wave of his trident, Neptune holds out a hand to help the woman into the chariot. Hand in hand, they sit close together, her long dress flowing from one side of the chariot, his jewel-encrusted tail lying over the other side.

The dolphins lift the reins and the chariot glides silently off, taking its royal owners away to begin their married life together.

Chapter One

*E*mily! I won't tell you again.' I opened an eye to see Mum pulling back the curtain across the porthole in my bedroom. Outside, an oval moon hung low in a navy sky. Fourth quarter, I thought automatically. We'd been learning about the moon's cycle at school. 'It's still night,' I complained as I pulled the quilt over my face and snuggled back into my pillow.

'It's half past seven,' Mum replied, perching on the edge of my bed. She folded the quilt back and kissed my forehead. 'Come on, sweet pea,' she said. 'You'll be late for school.' As she got up, she added under her breath, 'Not that you'd miss much if you were. They haven't exactly taught you anything useful at that place so far.'

She'd left the room before I had a chance to reply.

I let out a heavy sigh as I lay in bed, looking up at the ceiling. Mum seemed to be really down lately. That was the third time she'd grumbled about something in the last week. Personally, I couldn't see what there was to complain about. We were living on a beautiful secret island: Mum, Dad and me, all together on an elegant old wooden ship, half sunk in the golden sand and sparkling water that surrounded the whole island. Merfolk and humans together in peace.

I realise that last bit isn't necessarily a requirement in everyone's ideal living situation, but it comes in handy when your mum's a human, your dad's a merman and you're half and half.

I pulled on my swimming costume and joined Mum at the breakfast table. As with everything else in our home, the table lay on a slant, so I held on to my cereal bowl as I ate.

Dad swam up to the trapdoor next to my seat and pulled himself up to kiss me on the cheek. 'Morning, my little starfish,' he said with a smile. 'Ready for your

Ocean Studies test?'

'Test me!' I said.

Dad scratched his head. 'How big can a Giant Japanese Spider Crab grow?'

'Three metres,' I said instantly.

'Very good. Hm. What colour is a banded butterfly fish?'

'Black and silver. Too easy!'

'Too pointless, more like,' Mum said under her breath. What was *wrong* with her?

Dad turned to her with a frown. 'Not again!' he sighed. 'What is the matter with you? Don't you want our daughter to do well at school?'

'I'm sorry,' she said, reaching down for Dad's hand. 'It's just . . .'

'What? What is it? She's learning lots, she's enjoying herself, getting good grades. I couldn't be more proud.' Dad winked at me as he talked. I smiled back.

Dad and I hadn't got on all that well when we first came to Allpoints Island. I mean, we didn't get on badly; it just wasn't easy. I'd spent most of my life without him and we didn't really know what to talk about, or where to start.

I didn't know he existed at all till recently. It was only a few months ago I'd even found out about myself – that I became a mermaid when I went in water. It terrified me to begin with. The first time it happened, I didn't know what was going on. It was in a school swimming lesson, of all places. But then I got used to it, and I'd sneak out to swim in the sea at night. That's how I met my best friend, Shona. She's a mermaid too. A proper full-time one. She helped me find my dad. Best day of my life, that was, when I sneaked into Neptune's prison and saw him for the first time.

I guess it all took a bit of getting used to. But the last few weeks had been brilliant, once all the trouble with the kraken was sorted. That's the most horrific, fearsome sea monster in the world, and I accidentally woke it up! Since then, Dad and I had been out swimming together every day, exploring the golden seabed around Allpoints Island; racing against the multi-coloured fish that filled every stretch of sea round here; playing tag in among the coral. Dad was officially the BEST dad in the world.

'That's just it,' Mum was saying. '*You* couldn't be more proud. And you've every right to feel proud. Yes, Emily's coming on leaps and bounds in . . .' She paused to reach over to the pile of textbooks I'd brought home the previous day. I *loved* all my school-books. They weren't like any schoolbooks I'd ever had before, that's for sure! For one thing, they were all made from the coolest shiny materials, or woven with seaweed and decorated with shells and pearls. And for another, they were in the swishiest subjects! School had never been such fun.

'. . . in *Seas and Sirens*,' Mum read from the top one. She picked out a couple more books from the pile.

'Or *Sailing and Stargazing*, or *Hair Braiding for Modern Mermaids*. I mean!'

'You mean what?' Dad asked, his voice coming out pinched and tight. 'Why shouldn't she learn about these things? It's her heritage. What exactly don't you like about it, Mary?'

That's when I knew something was really wrong. No one *ever* calls my mum Mary, least of all Dad. Most people call her Mary P. Her middle name's Penelope and Dad's always called her Penny, or his lucky Penny when they're being particularly gooey. Which they hadn't been for a while, now I thought about it. And while I was thinking about it, I guess Mum had a point. I mean, don't get me wrong. I loved all my school subjects. But maybe I did sometimes miss my old school subjects, just a tiny bit. Or just English, perhaps. I used to love writing stories. I even liked spelling tests! That's just because I was good at them.

'What's wrong,' said Mum, 'is that while *you* may be happy for *your* daughter to learn nothing more than how to brush her hair nicely and tell the time by looking at the clouds, *I'd* like *my* daughter to get a proper education.'

'My daughter, your daughter? You make it sound as if she's two different people,' Dad said. Below the floor I could see the water swishing round as he swirled his tail angrily. It splashed up on to the kitchen floor.

'Yes, well, maybe she is,' Mum snapped, picking up

a tea towel and bending down to wipe the floor. Then she glanced up at me and her face softened. 'I mean, of course she's not. She's not two different people at all. It's not Emily's fault.' Mum smiled at me, reaching up to take hold of my hands. I snatched them away, turning my face at the same time so I couldn't see the hurt look in her eyes. That's one thing I absolutely can't stand.

But it wasn't fair. She wasn't being fair. I'd never enjoyed school this much in my life! And OK, so maybe it would be nice to write stories sometimes, but so what if I wasn't learning languages and logarithms or fractions and French? Who said there was any point in those either? Was I ever really going to need to know how much John earns in a week if he gets 4% commission and 3% interest? Surely learning about my surroundings was more important? Knowing which fish were the most dangerous and which were almost friendly. Learning how to look and act like other mermaids, like *proper* mermaids. Even if I did feel a bit silly perching on a rock combing my hair sometimes, at least I was learning how to fit in. Didn't Mum care about those things? Didn't she want me to be happy?

I carried on eating my breakfast.

Mum drew a breath. 'It's just that it's two different worlds,' she said in a quiet voice. 'And I sometimes wonder if they're simply *too* different. I mean, look at my life here. What do I do all day? Sunbathe, comb my hair, maybe go to Synchro Swim a couple of times a week. This isn't a life for me, Jake. I want more than this.'

No one spoke for ages. Mum and Dad stared at each other. I'd just taken a spoonful of cereal and didn't want to chew in case it crunched really loudly, so I sat there with my mouth full of cornflakes and milk, waiting for one of them to say something.

'We'll talk about this later. I need to go out,' Dad said eventually and I swallowed my mouthful. It was too soggy to chew anyway.

Dad left so quickly he didn't even give me a kiss. Not that I was bothered. I mean, I am twelve. I'll be thirteen in a couple of months. It's not as if I need my dad to kiss me goodbye when he goes out!

But. Well, it showed something. Maybe this was all my fault. It was only because of me that they had to try to bring the two worlds together at all. That and the fact that they loved each other, of course. But maybe they didn't any more. Maybe they'd grown away from each other so much in the twelve years they'd been apart that they didn't love each other at all now, and just had to stay together because of me. And they both hated it, and hated each other, and in the end they'd both end up hating me, too. And now, Mum didn't even like her life any more!

A strange cold feeling started to spread inside me, creeping around my body, seeping into my bones. Only weeks ago, we'd been given a new start on this island. A dream come true. Everything we'd ever wanted. But maybe it wasn't a dream come true at all. Maybe it was going to turn into a nightmare, like so many of my dreams did. Or used to.

Perhaps it was only a matter of time before Mum and Dad decided to abandon ship and not bother being together at all. Then what? Would I have to choose between them? Would either of them even want me if it was all because of me that their marriage had gone wrong? They'd probably fight each other *not* to have me.

I tried to shake the thoughts from my mind as I got ready for school. The Ocean Studies test was this afternoon and I was determined to do well. I'd show Dad that I really could follow in his footsteps, or wash in his wake, as he liked to say.

The thought cheered me up and I even allowed myself to smile as I packed my books. Till another thought chased the smile off my face like a shark chasing off a shoal of unsuspecting barjacks.

The more I did well in my mermaid lessons, the less time I was spending on land with Mum, doing what she liked. The closer I got to Dad, the further away I moved from her. Now I thought about it, I wasn't surprised she was unhappy. I'd been so busy getting to know Dad, I'd hardly done anything with Mum.

Perhaps she was right after all. Perhaps the two worlds were simply too different to coexist. Perhaps my parents weren't meant to be together at all.

I slunk away from the boat, dropping into the water without even saying goodbye, too miserable to speak, too scared to think.

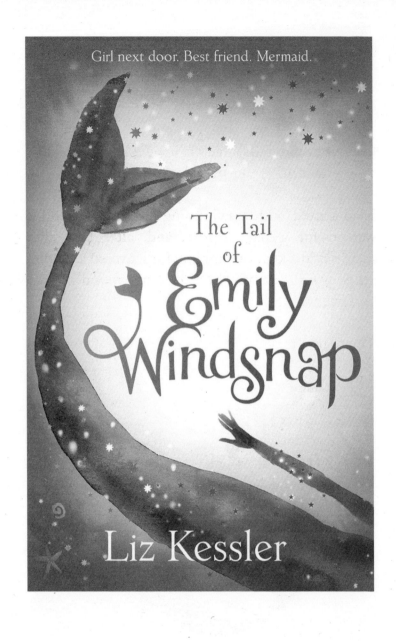

Girl next door. Best friend. Mermaid.

The Tail
of
Emily
Windsnap

Liz Kessler

Can you keep a secret?

I know everyone has secrets but mine's different. I mean, how many mermaids do you know?

It all started with a swimming lesson at school. I was in for a big surprise, and, after that, the surprises just kept on coming. I discovered a whole other world beneath the waves and found a new best friend.

This is my story.

Swishy wishes,

Emily Windsnap

Emily Windsnap and the Castle in the Mist

When I found a ring buried in the sand, I couldn't resist trying it on. I didn't know it would drive King Neptune into such a rage that he'd send my boat spinning across the ocean. Luckily my best friend, Shona Silkfin, was there to keep me company. We wanted to know the story of the ring and the secret of the magical castle that we could see shimmering in the mist. Wouldn't you?

Swishy wishes,

Emily Windsnap

Emily Windsnap and the Siren's Secret

Do you ever feel like you're going crazy?

That's how I was feeling after our return to Brightport. Everything seemed perfect but deep down I knew something was wrong. When I was thrown out of mermaid school, I decided I would go in search of the sirens, banished by Neptune to a top secret undersea cavern.

And when I did, I discovered an amazing story . . .

Swishy wishes,

Emily Windsnap and the Land of the Midnight Sun

Have you ever had nightmares?

King Neptune has, and that's why he sent me on a top secret mission.

When I discovered a kingdom with everyone turned to ice, I knew why the nightmares had terrified him. I needed help to complete my mission, but my best friend, Shona, was miles away and my boyfriend, Aaron, had just told me a secret that left us barely speaking. The question was, could we work together to save our world – and our relationship?

Swishy wishes,

Emily Windsnap and the Ship of Lost Souls

When I headed to Fivebays Island with both of my schools, I thought it would be an ordinary trip – well, as ordinary as it could be with humans and merpeople side by side!

But I soon realised something wasn't right. Where was the woman who'd invited us? Why did her husband seem so uneasy? And why did an old-fashioned ship keep appearing and vanishing out in the bay?

I could tell a new adventure was sneaking up on me!

Swishy wishes,

If you enjoyed Emily Windsnap . . .

MISSING: one arm
PROPERTY OF: Jessica Jenkins
LAST SEEN: Miss Cooper's geography lesson, Friday afternoon, connected to Jessica's shoulder.

Jessica Jenkins used to be ordinary, but now she can do things that aren't exactly normal – like turning invisible without even thinking about it!

Her best friend, Izzy, is excited – but is it all fun and games? Having a secret superpower can be dangerous! Where has Jessica's ability come from? And what happens if the wrong people find out what she can do?

Fun, friendship and superpowers from bestselling *Emily Windsnap* author, Liz Kessler.